"I Don't Like Name Games

"What's your position with the Logan conglomerate, Mr. Boone?"

Ethan frowned at her tone of voice. Gone was the endearing woman who'd captured his imagination, and in her place was this curt, businesslike creature.

"Try chief executive officer, Logan Tobacco," he answered, his voice authoritative.

She shut her eyes for a moment, then said quietly, "I'm Tara Ross."

He stared at her. "Oh, God," he said in frustration. "I don't believe this. We need to talk," he ordered. "Right now. I think you owe me that, after what you did last week."

"You talk, and I'll take notes," she answered coolly.

"But the question is, will you really listen?"

"Oh, yes. I'm fascinated by people who have no conscience."

He assessed her with the shrewd, respectful gaze of a man who enjoys a strong opponent. Her eyes returned the challenge.

Dear Reader:

Welcome! You hold in your hand a Silhouette Desire—your ticket to a whole new world of reading pleasure.

A Silhouette Desire is a sensuous, contemporary romance about passions, problems and the ultimate power of love. It is about today's woman—intelligent, successful, giving—but it is also the story of a romance between two people who are strong enough to follow their own individual paths, yet strong enough to compromise, as well.

These books are written by, for and about every woman that you are—wife, mother, sister, lover, daughter, career woman. A Silhouette Desire heroine must face the same challenges, achieve the same successes, in her story as you do in your own life.

The Silhouette reader is not afraid to enjoy herself. She knows when to take things seriously and when to indulge in a fantasy world. With six books a month, Silhouette Desire strives to meet her many moods, but each book is always a compelling love story.

Make a commitment to romance—go wild with Silhouette Desire!

Best,

Isabel Swift
Senior Editor & Editorial Coordinator

JACQUELYN LENNOX
Force of Habit

Silhouette Desire

Published by Silhouette Books New York

America's Publisher of Contemporary Romance

SILHOUETTE BOOKS
300 East 42nd St., New York, N.Y. 10017

Copyright © 1988 by Deborah Smith

ISBN: 0-373-05429-7

First Silhouette Books printing June 1988

JACQUELYN LENNOX

is a dedicated daydreamer who carries on animated conversations with herself, usually while driving. She developed this habit when she worked as a newspaper reporter and then as a medical writer, two jobs that allowed little outlet for her romantic fantasies or creativity.

She and her engineer husband first met in high school, where each decided that the other was too bossy. Romance blossomed several years later. Now they're arguing happily over the construction of a home in the north Georgia mountains.

To Jack, Rena, Chris and Rachel

One

His stomach had already turned into a painful knot of old griefs even before he lifted his eyes from the walkway and gazed at the solemn black granite of the monument. The ebony stone shimmered under fine tears of rain from the soggy spring day, and the dull sky promised to polish the monument's slick surface again before dusk settled.

Ethan Boone flipped up the lapels on his finely tailored raincoat and tried to breath normally. Nothing in his imaginings about this much-publicized place had prepared him for the overwhelming sensation of awe that slid up his spine, mingled with a sharp prickle of horror. His elder brother had died, violently and uselessly, and here stretched the incontrovertible truth that he would never come home.

Ethan dimly heard the measured, sturdy sound of his footsteps as he approached the stark monument, its black wings sunk in a grassy bank as if it were an abstract angel trying to rise to heaven. He knew if he looked over his shoulder he could see the Lincoln Memorial shrouded in the fog that was creeping off the Potomac River. He knew if he listened he could hear the rush-hour traffic on Constitution Avenue. Those things didn't matter, because he couldn't look away and he couldn't hear anything except the hard thumping of his own heart.

He reached the gleaming wall and touched his fingertips to its surface, feeling the scars of the names. The harsh tide of emotions that rushed over him was unfamiliar, disconcerting to a man who prided himself on being in control at all times.

Within ten minutes he found his brother. While his fingers traced each letter of the name, Ethan cursed viciously and softly until his throat closed and he could do no more than simply stand still, aching, staring at the name of the young Southerner who should have been alive on this April day to celebrate being forty-two years old.

A soft, muffled sound slid under Ethan's veil of depression and captured his attention with its heartbroken tone. Startled, because a few minutes ago he'd been alone in the memorial park, he quickly swiveled his head toward the source.

She stood at the glistening wall two dozen feet away, her slender body angled so that he could see only the back of her camel-colored raincoat and the damp waves of her short brunette hair. Ethan watched her left hand slip forward and touch a name on the wall with the same reverence he had used. She cupped her right hand over her face and her shoulders quivered. Again he heard the quiet, resonant murmur of her grief.

He understood that grief as if she had communicated it to him telepathically, searching out the compassion of a kindred soul. Ethan dropped his hand to his side, then clenched it in frustration. He took a step toward her, then stopped. Ordinarily indecision was foreign to him, but now it held him in its grasp, as insistent as the rest of his jumbled emotions.

Would she be frightened if he walked over to her? he wondered. They were the only two people here—the only two people in the world, it seemed—and he frowned as he considered her recklessness. Why was she alone here? Even in this section of D.C., a woman had no business wandering around by herself near dark.

With that oddly intense feeling of protectiveness, Ethan stepped forward. He stopped again when she straightened and brushed at her face, her hands fumbling but also exquisitely graceful. She reached into the sleek leather purse that hung by her side and retrieved something.

Ethan's breath caught as she unwrapped white tissue paper from a tiny, ragged-looking cloth doll. He gazed in wonder as she stooped in one fluid motion and laid the doll at the base of the monument wall. Others had left flowers here—they did so every day, he'd read in a newspaper account somewhere—and the colorful bouquets lined the wall with all the wistful beauty of funeral dressings.

But that doll—a cherished toy from her childhood?—did more to unhinge the remnants of his sadness than he'd expected, and Ethan ducked his head, eyes closed in a grim attempt to draw his reserve back together, feeling more vulnerable than he had in years.

Tara Ross turned around without knowing why. She had the uncanny feeling that she was being watched by the well-dressed man who'd been standing with his back to her moments ago. Her hands froze around her face as she saw him with his head down, his eyes closed, almost as if he were in prayer. The sight ripped at her sympathy at the same time that it intrigued her.

He presented a dramatic picture in a classic trench coat, which had fallen open in the center to reveal a double-breasted black suit with pinstripes. His hair was thick and stylishly cut, a beautiful mixture of blonds disrupted by the wind's fingers. He leaned lightly on a closed black umbrella.

Tara realized that she wasn't breathing steadily and didn't know whether to attribute her agitation to the torment she'd felt from looking at her father's name on the wall or to the mesmerizing man who seemed even more distraught than she was. She saw him sigh, then shift his weight as if he'd just learned how to shoulder some inner burden.

Tara caught her lower lip with her teeth and wheeled around a split second before his eyes opened. She knew dearly the value of privacy, and she gave him his. Fumbling in her purse, she found a tissue and began to dab wearily at her face.

The first huge drops of rain struck her hand and the tissue, soaking the thin paper. Tara looked up at the gray sky and caught more wetness on her face. The rain, with only that warning, began to cascade down in sheets.

Tara gasped, jabbed the tissue into her pocket and pulled the lapels of her raincoat tightly around her neck even as she felt her hair slicking to her scalp. She could hardly see, and she took two uncertain steps forward, shielding her eyes as best she could with her free hand.

"Please," she heard a deep voice say. And before she realized that he had walked over to her, the stranger covered her with the wide protection of his open umbrella.

Tara shivered and instinctively moved away. He followed with a single step, not touching her, but so close that she caught the fragrance of good cologne mixed with a scent that was overtly damp and masculine.

"Please," he said again, his voice low and melodic. "I'm trustworthy, and you're soaked."

He said those words with a touch of humor overlying a sadness that echoed her own. Tara looked up at him—a good deal up, for he was much taller than she was—and managed a slight smile.

"I'm assuming that you're trustworthy. I'm certain that I'm soaked." She paused, letting her gaze flow over rugged features, which were a bit too strong, but handsome. "Thank you."

Tara looked away, dimly aware that she had cataloged a stubborn jaw and a wide, serious mouth under amazing blue eyes. And his voice—it had been magnificent, with a cultured Southern drawl to it. He leaned toward her an inch and spoke loudly to overcome the heavy patter of rain on the umbrella.

"We'd better just stay here until it slacks up. There's no point in walking into it when it's whipping like this. At least here by the monument we have a little protection."

She nodded and reached in her pocket for her tissue. Tara folded its soggy width into a tiny, usable square and began wiping her cheeks, glad that the raindrops had camouflaged her tears. The man beside her quickly reached inside his coat and produced a linen handkerchief.

"Here." His voice was so gentle that she looked up in surprise. She found sympathy and concern in his eyes, then realized that her crying hadn't escaped his notice. She frowned and stiffened as new tears welled up inside her, drawn to the surface by this stranger's disturbing and caring presence. Tara blinked rapidly, took the handkerchief and stared hard into the silver rain. With every rigid muscle in her body and her face she fought the tears that slid, heedless, over her lashes and down her cheeks. She heard him inhale raggedly.

"I'm very sorry," he told her, and her silent tears came faster. Tara quivered with restraint. "If I can help...if you'll let me . . . I believe we're in this together . . ."

She closed her eyes, unable to answer without losing all her control. His long arm slid around her back with a powerful and graceful motion, and his hand cupped snugly around her arm on the opposite side.

Tara's common sense told her that the wisest way to respond to this stranger in a deserted park was to move away; her tattered emotions told her to move closer to a source of comfort. She lacked comfort in her life, and the umbrella demanded closeness, so she followed her emotions.

"I understand how you feel," he murmured. "It affected me the same way. This is the first time I've been here. How about you?"

"First time."

Ethan exhaled slowly as her shoulder settled into the crook of his, the rest of her not touching him. He looked fixedly at the pouring rain, swallowed hard, then looked down at her as she bent her head and pressed his handkerchief over her eyes.

I could look at her forever, he thought. She had a sturdy beauty in her face, not the fine-boned look of a model, and her hair was a sleek chocolate shade cut in fashionable layers that ended before they reached her shoulders. Just now it was plastered to her head, but tendrils escaped here and there to curl against skin the color of vanilla with gold undertones. She was enchanting.

"I lost a brother," he told her gruffly. "An older brother. Today would have been his forty-second birthday."

She made a soft sound of sorrow on his behalf. "I lost my father. I was about twelve when he died, and I can't believe this is affecting me so badly almost two decades later. I feel foolish."

"This place has a certain power about it. I didn't think it would bother me at all, until I got here." Ethan took a tired breath. "I was wrong."

The rain continued to drench everything around them. She smoothed his handkerchief over her face one last time, inhaling his cologne from the fine material. She politely folded the white sheet and offered it to him, then realized that he didn't have a free hand. His eyes met hers with a look that seemed teasing.

"I can't take that back," he quipped, his voice a little hoarse. "It has mascara on it. What would my mother think if she saw it?"

A gentle sound that verged on laughter escaped Tara's lips. This man's mother was used to much more scandalous things from her son; of that she felt certain. "I can't keep it," she told him wryly. "It smells of a man's cologne. What would *my* mother think?"

He smiled, not widely—she had the feeling his serious mouth didn't allow for large, gratuitous smiles—but warmly, revealing blocky white teeth that complemented his rugged face by being not quite perfect. He wouldn't look as appealing with a capped-and-crowned smile, she decided with a measure of proprietorship. She liked him human. She liked him, period.

"Your mother," he said. "Does she approve of you wandering around parks alone?"

She tilted one brow at his somewhat disapproving tone of voice. "In the interest of destroying your paternal attitude, I ask you the same question about your mother."

"Point taken. But I'm hardly being paternal. Macho and protective, maybe. How about that?" he teased her with an arched brow.

"Macho and protective are all right, I suppose."

He smiled, then shifted his body, a movement that suggested to her wandering eyes that the shoulders under his coat were very well developed. She felt his arm pressing tighter across her back and the subtle squeeze of his fingers fitting more snugly around her arm. She began to feel pleasantly warm.

"It's unusual for this park to be deserted," he murmured. "From what I've read about the monument, I expected to find more people here."

"I didn't know what to expect." She turned newly solemn eyes toward the wet vista of spring greenery before them. The rain continued to crash down, splashing against her low-heeled pumps and molding her wet hose to her ankles. Tara shivered, and after a moment he stepped closer so that the length of his side was against her. Tara assured herself that with the bulky raincoats between them there was nothing wrong with letting her body press tighter to his.

"It's beautiful here, even today," he said in a distracted voice. "In a way that makes a person hurt. It's too beautiful."

She wondered if, like her, he was considering the way their bodies fitted together so well. "Yes." Neither of them said anything for a moment. Then Tara ventured, "Your brother. Tell me about him."

"He was a marine. Nineteen years old. He was in Vietnam only a couple of months before he was killed by a mine."

"He was an older brother, you said?"

"Four years."

"That must have been very hard for you to take, since you were so young at the time."

He nodded, and she watched a muscle flex in his jaw. Tara studied his profile, her curiosity aroused by the details of this stranger's life. His face was mature and weathered, with character lines around those magnetic blue eyes and a hint of handsome creases on either side of his mouth. His nose was sturdy and attractively crooked, his cheekbones high.

"Was he your only brother?"

Ethan turned his head to gaze down at her with surprise. Her gentle prodding seemed motivated by more than politeness; she really seemed to care. Affection added fuel to the glow of physical attraction he'd felt the moment he'd seen her face.

"No. I have a younger brother." He nodded slightly, as if giving her a slight bow of introduction. "In Kentucky. We were born there. I migrated north."

"I knew you were Southern, from your accent. It's marvelous. As a plain old Midwesterner, I envy it."

"You're neither plain nor old," he countered. Ethan assessed the fine laugh lines around her eyes, eyes that he now, finally, had a chance to study. Green and sheltered by dark lashes, they were large and soulful. They seemed to hold a reservoir of sorrow behind them.

He wanted to see her laugh, to see the sadness in her eyes disappear and the laugh lines deepen. Her eyes snapped with intelligence, and that fact combined with her soul-stirring face to make his mind go blank for a moment.

"Why, thank you," she answered with a touch of self-deprecating dryness in her voice. "But I'm about to turn thirty-one. It bothers me to realize that in a few years I'll be of almost no demographic interest to the editors of *Seventeen* magazine."

Her teasing, sardonic humor charmed him. He repressed a smile.

Tara felt her eyes widening, and her stomach dropped languidly as she gazed up at his disarming expression. She read the unconcealed interest there and realized abruptly that she was returning it. She looked away, a guilt pang tugging at her conscience.

Somewhere in a harsh, strife-torn part of the world, a tortured man might be clinging desperately to memories of her, and she owed him loyalty in return for the love they'd once shared. Until today, maintaining that loyalty had been no problem. Until today, and this provocative blond stranger. Tara cleared her throat and narrowed her eyes to shut out the sight of him beside her, so close beside her.

"The rain's stopping," she murmured. "I'll let you have your umbrella back to yourself. I can never thank you enough."

"I... Don't leave," he said quickly. Tara swung a startled look in his direction and caught fleeting awkwardness in his eyes just before gruff reserve covered it. "You can't leave without telling me about your father. What branch of the service was he in?"

"The Air Force. He was a pilot." She kept her voice low and neutral, determined to trap her emotions where they belonged—out of this man's sharp sight. "He was shot down during his third tour of duty, a week before he was scheduled to come home."

She turned, her movement forcing Ethan to drop his arm from around her back, and studied the monument wall with tormented eyes. His gaze shifted from her face to the column of names, and he started to ask her which was her father's. Afterward he would find out her name. Then he would ask her to dinner.

"The rain's stopped. I have to go," she interjected abruptly, and, swinging about on her heel, stepped away from him. Ethan blinked rapidly and looked up at the traitorous skies in search of the rain that had just deserted him. "Thank you again," she murmured.

"Let me walk you to the street."

He took her arm firmly and popped the umbrella closed. Tara looked up at him in pure dismay. He had a no-nonsense air about him now—a confident, determined attitude—even though she thought she'd made it clear that she didn't want to talk to him any longer. He met her eyes and gave no ground. "You shouldn't walk here alone," he said.

"It isn't that far to the street, you know."

"Then you'll have to put up with my macho protection for only another minute or two."

Tara's mouth opened in embarrassment. "I didn't mean it that way," she lied. "I'm sure that you have someplace you need to be going, and I don't want to bother you anymore."

"It's no bother."

She saw a hint of disappointment under his shield of nonchalance, and it touched her. She smiled at him quizzically. "Are you playing guardian angel, then?"

"Yes."

His staunch, unhesitant answer rattled her. She burned with a combination of anxiety about the personal turn this chance meeting had taken and undeniable pleasure at his protective attitude. She'd had no one for so long, and needed someone for so long, that this amazing stranger provided a dangerous temptation. No. No.

She started to warn him that she wasn't looking for a guardian angel or a personal relationship, but before she got the words out he looked away from her, toward the monument. Tara's words died in her throat as she watched him silently saying his goodbye. Her chest aching with new torment, she silently added her own. It belonged to a wistful twelve-year-old who had never quite gotten over her father's death. *Goodbye, Daddy. I love you.*

"Enough," the man beside her said softly. Tara realized that she was under his gaze again, that he had once again been privy to her emotions. Suddenly weary, she looked up at him with no defense. They shared their old wounds for a moment, their eyes locked. "Come on. Let's get out of here," he added kindly, and pressed on her arm to direct her up the walkway. "I've had almost all I can stand of this, and I think you have, too."

She nodded, thinking that those words applied not only to this moment in her life but to the past two years. They walked slowly toward bustling Constitution Avenue, a companionable silence stretching between them.

"I feel an attack of blunt curiosity coming on," he said finally. "Are you married?"

Tara couldn't help smiling at his smooth candor. "No."

"Ah, bluntness always works so well." He chuckled. "Engaged? Attached? Embroiled with a 'significant other'? Promised to a convent? Celibate—"

"I think we should just leave it at 'unmarried,'" she interjected, laughing to cover the anxiety that welled up inside her.

"Good enough." He nodded in gallant acceptance, his manner almost courtly. The man was undoubtedly an expert at charming information from people, Tara concluded. She herself was skilled at diplomatic snooping, so she could appreciate his ability, even if it unnerved her.

When he and Tara exited the park and stood on the sidewalk, they faced the Federal Reserve Board building and the National Academy of Sciences across the avenue. Rush-hour traffic sped by and pedestrians poured around them in a steady stream.

"Welcome back to civilization," she muttered ruefully. He smiled and nodded to convey his own dismay.

"I don't want to jump back into the rat race," he told her. Ethan paused, gathering his forces. He had no problem with women, no awkwardness about asking for what he wanted, and very little trouble getting it. None of that made any difference right now, however, because he felt like a nervous teenager. "Look, if you're as tired and hungry as I am, why don't you share a taxi with me, and dinner?"

Tara absorbed his calm, unwavering gaze and knew she was in the presence of a master strategist. Everything about him whispered that he was a success in any area he chose to enter. The idea of becoming one of those areas herself held definite temptations.

"I'm sorry—" she began.

"Ah!" He held up a forefinger and smiled, warning her to stop. "I shouldn't ask until after we've been formally introduced. I know that."

The look in his eyes could woo birds from the trees, she thought desperately.

"You can't refuse until *after* we're introduced," he added.

Despite herself, she smiled at his resourcefulness. She did want to know his name, so that she could carry it with her when she stepped into a taxi and went her own way. His name was something harmless she could enjoy.

"All right, let's get to it," she quipped. "You first."

He nodded, still smiling, and extended his right hand. She grasped it, and they traded firm grips. The warmth and hardness of his palm were disturbing in a pleasant way.

"Ethan Boone, from New York, here on business for Logan Tobacco," he said slowly, emphasizing each word.

Tara's hand jerked slightly as shock poured into her fingers. It couldn't be. He couldn't be from Logan. For a second she stared at him with utter disbelief growing on her face, and then she pulled her hand away. He gave her a bewildered look.

"What do you do for Logan Tobacco?" she asked as calmly as she could. Now she thought she could smell a faint, rich cigar scent on him. She almost grimaced. "Do you actually work for Logan Tobacco, or for one of the companies that Logan owns?"

"I'm not a janitor, if that's what you're worrying about." His eyes teased her. "I'm a mail boy."

She responded with a frown to his attempt at humor.

"Boone. Boone. I know your name, but I just can't place it with a job title, and I've written a lot about your company."

"I'm a distant relative of Daniel's, but I doubt that's what you mean. I've been with Logan only a short time. Maybe that's why you haven't heard of me. Are you from New York, too?"

"Yes."

"Well, I was quoted in that liberal rag *The New York Constitution* last week. Perhaps that's where you saw my name, though I'd hate to think that you read that fish wrapper."

Tara's mouth clamped into a grim line at his assessment of the *Constitution*.

"I don't like name games. What's your position with the Logan conglomerate, Mr. Boone?"

He frowned at her tone of voice. Gone was the endearing woman who'd captured his imagination, and in her place was a curt, businesslike creature.

"Try Chief Executive Officer, Logan Tobacco," he answered, his voice authoritative.

She shut her eyes for a moment. When she opened them, he saw that they were almost apologetic.

"I'm Tara Ross," she said quietly. Her voice was laced with regret and anger and underneath that, bitter disappointment that he had just ruined the fantasies she'd planned to carry away with her. She took a step back and stiffened her shoulders. "I'm the health and science editor for that 'fish wrapper' you just mentioned."

Ethan's lips parted and he stared at her, speechless. The poker face he thought he'd nurtured so well for business situations failed him for a moment. *Why her?*

"Oh, God," he said in frustration. "I don't believe this."

Dismay darkened his eyes, and Tara was surprised that she felt hurt to see it directed at her. The man who'd shared his grief with her at the memorial now looked as if he could perform ruthless acts without guilt. And had done so, from what she knew about the company.

"We need to talk," he ordered, his expression suffused with anger. "Right now. After what my sources told me that you did last week, I think you owe me that."

"You talk, and I'll take notes," she answered coolly.

"But the question is, will you really listen?"

"Oh, yes. I'm fascinated by people who have no conscience."

He assessed her with the shrewd, respectful gaze of a man who enjoys a strong opponent. With her eyes she returned the challenge.

Two

Where you go?'' the cabdriver asked in an Oriental accent, his face distorted as if the strain of speaking a new language were still too much. The irony that he might be Vietnamese wasn't lost on Tara, and when she glanced at Ethan, she found him smiling sardonically. For just one second their differences were forgotten again as they traded a look of amusement. Then the mood was gone. Tara held up a hand toward the driver.

"Give us just a moment, please."

"No wait, lady. Traffic bad. Hurry."

Ethan jabbed the point of his umbrella into the floor between him and Tara, symbolically marking a dividing line in the cab's back seat. He made a small shrug.

"Your choice," he told her curtly. "I don't care where we talk, as long as we get some points settled." She nodded in grim and silent acceptance, then fastened her gaze on the driver.

"The Democrat," she told him. "It's over near Capitol Hill."

"I know where, lady," he answered in disgust. "I take two senators there yesterday."

With that he burned rubber into traffic. The jerking motion of the clumsy yellow cab threw Tara against Ethan's arm. Instinctively he reached across his body and steadied her, his hand on her elbow, and just as instinctively she flattened one hand against his shoulder.

With her other hand she also reached for his shoulder but missed and slid across his chest, stopping only when she grasped it on the lapel of his coat. Their faces inches apart, they shared a direct and startled gaze, blue eyes burning into green.

"I'm sorry.... Excuse me," she said quickly, and couldn't hide the evidence of embarrassment creeping up her cheeks. *Too close, too close,* her inner voice reported in alarm. Too much power. Too much confusing feedback.

His jaw tightened. His hand held her elbow firmly. Tara pressed backward, away from the wide, strong grip and the gleam that rose in his eyes. She couldn't move to her side of the cab without jerking her arm out of his clasp, and she had an ironclad rule never to lose her cool in an interview. She hovered on the verge of breaking the hell out of that rule.

"You like to make people squirm," he told her softly. "How does it feel when the tables are turned?"

She pursed her lips as she considered a smooth answer. Ethan's eyes were drawn to them, and he wondered what insanity made him find her even more provocative now that he'd identified her as a problem. Worried about his reaction to her, he abruptly let go of her arm.

"If I make people squirm, it's because they deserve it," she told him, her voice taut. Tara settled in her seat and exhaled slowly. But, still rigid with tension, she faced forward and knotted her hands over the burgundy purse in her lap.

"Who gave you those confidential memos last week?" he demanded.

"You know I can't answer that."

"When do you plan to publish them?"

"As soon as I've checked out some of the details for accuracy."

"And then you'll barbecue the poor bastards who wrote them."

Tara shook her head in grim denial of his accusation. "I'll report the facts and let the readers decide who's at fault. I'm not... I'm not a monster, Mr. Boone. I don't like to hurt people." She paused, frowning. Why did Ethan Boone make her feel so guilty? "The people you're referring to knew what they'd encounter when they put themselves in indefensible positions. Researchers who have the audacity to say that tobacco isn't conclusively linked to disease deserve to be investigated. And when they admit their real beliefs in company memos, that's important news."

The cab lurched through the crowded streets of Washington, passing and being passed by glossy black limousines, standard sights in the high-powered city. Street lamps shimmered with the promise of light as evening closed in. Ethan rapped impatient fingers along the handle of his umbrella.

"You've written at least a dozen columns refuting our experts over the past two months," he said, keeping his voice smooth and calm, much more so than he felt. "Don't you have anything else to discuss in your health and science column? Aren't AIDS and artificial hearts still worth headlines? What vendetta have you got against my company?"

"It's professional, not personal," she answered sharply. "If I'm focusing on Logan Tobacco, it's because, of the three major cigarette manufacturers in this country, Logan is the only one that's begun an aggressive campaign to defend tobacco." She drew herself up calmly. "If you're going to sell toxic products, Mr. Boone, the least you can do is keep a low profile about it.''

Ethan laughed in a low, predatory way. "Spare me your righteous opinions, Ms. Ross. I don't need a lecture on virtue.''

He sank back in his seat and stared grimly out the cab window, wishing he could tell her the truth. Hell, he wished he could tell everyone the truth, but all he could do was mouth marketing platitudes and hope she'd print a few of them in the company's defense. He disliked the damned tobacco business. He knew the products hurt people.

He'd wanted to remain CEO of Allied Foods, one of the companies owned by Logan, but he hadn't had the choice. Last year Logan's board of directors had a desperate situation on their hands—fluctuating stock values, the growing public debate over smoking, slipping tobacco sales—and they recalled how he'd stabilized a critical situation at Allied. They made their position clear: if he didn't take the CEO position at Logan Tobacco, at least temporarily, he had no future with the Logan conglomerate.

"Let's talk about the congressional hearings," he said abruptly. "I'm in town to attend them, as you've probably already deduced. How do you think Logan Tobacco ought to respond? Can't the company protect itself the same way any legitimate corporation would when faced with the prospect of unfair trade restrictions?''

"Believe it or not, Mr. Boone, I don't like the proposal to ban tobacco advertising any better than you do. I don't think it would solve the problem, and being a journalist, I have a great deal of respect for freedom of speech. But that issue isn't in my domain. I write medical stories. I don't care if the public buys your products. I just want you to tell those people how dangerous they are.''

Ethan looked at her with surprise and then grudging respect. "Your objectivity is noted," he said slowly. "Thank you.''

A little flustered by his change in attitude, Tara stared silently across the darkening cab at him, watching the glow from the street lamps shoot golden streaks through his hair. He looked mysterious and untouchable as the shadows straightened themselves to the angles of his strong face. Even her anger couldn't destroy her sense of the pure virile magnetism that this man radiated. He returned her scrutiny with disturbing intensity. Tara looked away.

"But about the legislation . . ." she began.

"The restrictions called for on the bill being considered by the House subcommittee are ludicrous." He held up his fingers and began counting. "A ban on all tobacco product ads in newspapers, magazines, billboards, posters, signs, decals, et cetera. A ban on coupons and samples. A ban on sponsorship by tobacco firms. Logan sponsors two major golf tournaments. We underwrite regional theaters and art festivals. Who's going to be hurt the most by this ridiculous legislation?"

"Your stockholders," she answered quietly. "Aren't any of them worried that children and teenagers might be drawn into smoking by Logan's glamorous ads?"

"Look, dammit, we advertise to adults. We advertise to make people switch brands, not to lure them into smoking. I know you've heard that dozens of times, but it's true."

Without thinking, she muttered a basic barnyard assessment of his statement. He gave her a cool, rebuking look, and Tara grimaced. She didn't ordinarily resort to crude language, except for a few fine-tuned words in private.

That was another of her ironclad rules, like keeping her emotions hidden from the people she interviewed. Like not taking their anger personally. Now she'd broken all three rules because of Ethan Boone's effect on her senses.

"I apologize for my language," she muttered.

"Don't apologize. If you're playing with the big boys, you should talk like them."

"Petty sexism doesn't become you," she answered quietly. The wistful defense in her voice caught him short, made him cringe with self-rebuke.

"You're right," he said in a brusque voice. "I apologize."

"Thank you."

"I may be a tobacco ogre, but I'm not a sexist tobacco ogre," he added with the faintest trace of humor.

"I'm glad. I appreciate that, more than you know."

They rode in uncomfortable silence for several minutes. Ethan straightened the lapels of his raincoat with a quick, angry tug of both hands. How could she be so tough yet seem so fragile at the same time? he thought in exasperation. His anger was losing track, merging with curiosity and renewed affection.

"We here. Pay now," their cabdriver growled. "Eight dollar." Ethan glanced out at an unprepossessing place sandwiched between a parking lot and a graying structure of uncertain age. A royal-blue canopy emblazoned with The Democrat, Restaurant and Bar, Established 1942, covered the sidewalk from the curb to the institutional glass-and-steel door tucked a few steps below street level in the old, brick building.

"I suppose the Republicans have something similar, somewhere," he said under his breath.

"They do," Tara noted. "It's on the other side of the Hill. It's pretty pretentious compared to this, of course."

"If you're assuming that I'm a Republican, you're right. And I'm proud of it."

"Mr. Boone, if you think you'll be uncomfortable in a liberal arena, we can go somewhere—"

"We go wherever you like!" the driver interjected. "We go or you pay. Get out, but quick!"

"I'll get the fare," Ethan said sternly. Tara snapped her purse open even as he reached under his raincoat and retrieved a sleek wallet.

"No, I've got it," she reprimanded. "I can't let you pay my way. Newspaper ethics."

Ethan's fingers paused over a ten-dollar bill he'd just slipped from the wallet. This woman was going to be more difficult to deal with than he'd imagined.

"Fine," he said wryly, and put his money away. He couldn't help adding, "Newspaper ethics? You're certain the term's not an oxymoron—like *jumbo shrimp* or *plastic glass*?"

"Like *business ethics*?" she asked in a droll voice.

Ethan controlled the urge to smile at her slick rejoinder. He shoved his door open and stepped onto the curb. She slid across the seat and he extended a hand to her. Tara gazed at it, then up at his arched brows. This was a dare.

To say "No, thanks" and ignore the gesture would be childish. To accept it would be subtly submissive. She grasped his hand hard and felt the pressure returned by his strong fingers. He pulled her out of the cab a little too forcefully, she thought. She snatched her hand out of his and slammed the cab door shut just as he reached over to perform the action himself.

"Why, you're a feisty little thing, aren't you?" he said in patronizing tones, his jaw thrust forward.

"You like mind games." Tara drew herself to her full five feet seven inches. "Well, you can't manipulate me and you can't manipulate my newspaper, and if you're trying to, you're sure as hell going about it the wrong way."

Frowning, Ethan stared at her for a moment. "Why, of course," he said suddenly. He slapped his head with the heel of one hand, as if he'd just remembered something. "I should be devious, shouldn't I? Underhanded and suspect and full of plans to indoctrinate children into the evils of smoking so that my lurid conglomerate can increase its profits. I forgot to act like a stereotype. Pardon me."

"Are we here to bicker, or are we here to talk?"

With that she turned on her heel and went downstairs, her blue pumps clicking on the granite steps. She ran a careless hand through her hair, which was now curling into gentle, dark waves, and snatched the door open. Respect and frustration gleaming in his eyes, Ethan followed her.

The Democrat was a dark, masculine place cluttered with heavy wooden tables and plush chairs, some of advanced ages. Booths with rich red leather seats paraded around the perimeter. Ethan scanned walls lined with paintings, mostly of local monuments, and with framed photos of the famous and infamous who had settled deals and hatched plans here over the years.

"Smoking or nonsmoking?" a mellow-looking man in blue pinstripes asked.

Tara curled her lips in a rueful smile. "Nonsmoking."

"I'll grant you that this time," Ethan said, standing close beside her. "But I do smoke an occasional cigar. A disgusting, thick cigar, with no filter tip."

Tara turned her head slightly and glanced back at him as they followed the host to a dimly lit booth in one corner. "Some psychiatrists believe that men who smoke cigars are sexually insecure. They say the cigar is a phallic symbol."

"I'll have to get a bigger cigar, then," he said smoothly.

She considered that rebuttal with pleased surprise. Like most newspaper people, she had a keen appreciation of humor and, also like most newspaper people, appreciated humor in the midst of odd circumstances.

"Very good," she admitted.

"Thank you."

This is strange, very strange, Ethan thought. This conversation flip-flopped between animosity and camaraderie. He liked her. He disliked her. It was getting difficult to know where one feeling ended and another began. He wanted to help her with her coat but knew the situation didn't allow such obvious courtesy.

So he removed his quickly and folded it over his arm, then stood by the booth, refusing to sit until she'd done so first. Tara glanced at him out of the corner of her eye and raised one brow.

"Please, go ahead and sit. This isn't a social occasion," she murmured.

Tara shrugged her damp coat down her shoulders, revealing an unstructured blue jacket over a white, V-necked blouse with just enough lacework around the collar to keep it from being severely plain. The jacket parted to give evidence of a slender but well-curved body. She wore a loose, print skirt full of muted blues and whites.

Ethan thought she presented a very businesslike but very feminine picture, with simple gold hoops in her ears and a no-nonsense watch held on her wrist by a leather band. He glanced at her hands. No engagement ring.

"Men born and raised in Kentucky don't sit down before a lady sits down," he told her somberly.

"Perhaps I'm not a lady," she replied. Tara shook her coat, then looked around for a place to deposit it.

"Give it to me." Without waiting for a response, Ethan took it from her and folded it over his own, then laid both coats over the worn mahogany backboard on his side of the booth. "I'll treat you like a lady until you prove otherwise."

Tara nodded, smiled with frosty acceptance and sat down. He sat across from her. Her heart rate had not been near normal since the moment he'd placed his umbrella over her with his heartfelt, coaxing "Please" to soften her surprise. Now it bumped higher.

His clothes were expensive, probably custom-made, she thought. The tie he wore was a soft gray with a tiny black stripe to match his suit. He placed his large, capable-looking hands one on top of the other on the table and the white cuffs of his shirt peeked out, complementing the ruddy color of his skin.

"*Lady* is a sexist term," she told him belatedly.

"I like it anyway. Don't quibble over semantics."

Tara nodded. So the battle lines were still drawn. "Semantics are my life," she said dryly. She felt victorious when he suppressed a smile.

They ordered coffee with brandy on the side. After the waiter left, Tara reached into her purse and pulled out a small pad and a pen. She put a miniature tape recorder beside the pad and turned it on.

"If you say something that you want off the record, tell me," she explained. "Otherwise, whatever you say is fair game."

"What prompts you to hate my company so much? People want a product—we provide that product. We didn't cause the problem."

Tara gazed at him in surprise. "So you admit that you're a problem. Hmm. By the way, I'm the one who's supposed to ask the questions here."

"I don't like that rule. I refuse to play by it. Answer me."

She smiled and shook her head in disbelief. "You mean, do I have something personal in my background, like a parent who died of emphysema or a great-aunt who chewed tobacco until her teeth fell out?"

"Something like that."

"No, I'm afraid not. Anyone who's written about medical topics for as long as I have would have to be blind not to have seen all the statistics on smoking. And I have a degree in biology as well as journalism. I not only read the statistics; I understand them."

He leaned forward. "Very impressive," he told her sincerely. He paused, looked rakish. "I bet that you used to smoke. Smoke heavily, too. You talk like a convert."

Tara felt the color drain out of her face. She knew this man could decipher people—no one got to be chief executive officer of a major company without that skill—but she hadn't counted on her personal life being the focus of his tactics.

"I did smoke, once upon a time," she admitted calmly. "I quit four years ago. I quit cold turkey, and I've never had a cigarette since." Except at a party sometimes, when I bum one off a friend, she added silently. And during rough airplane flights.

"That's commendable. I congratulate you."

She gave that remark an "Oh, sure" look. "You wouldn't if you took time to figure out the revenues you've lost because of me. I smoked over two packs a day—Laramies, unfiltered. The short ones, the long ones, the mentholated ones, the ones in the designer packs, the ones in the plain old foil packs—any kind of Laramie cigarette Logan made, I smoked it."

"You like to take risks." Laramie was Logan Tobacco's premier brand, a cigarette for hard-core smokers who didn't give a damn about tar and nicotine ratings. "What made you quit so abruptly?"

"I like to breathe more than I like to take risks. And I'd just been promoted to health and science editor. It was bad for my image."

Tara looked down at her clasped hands. They were inches from his, and for a moment she idly studied the contrast between her small, delicate bone structure and his brawniness. It was a sensual picture, male and female hands in comparison.

"I suspect you quit for less noble reasons," Ethan told her. "Let's see. You had a man friend who objected to nicotine-flavored kisses."

Again, Tara was certain he wanted to smile but was hiding the urge. "I suspect," she replied sternly, "that we're off the subject of Logan Tobacco."

"No man friend?" he persisted.

Tara sighed. "Yes, a man friend. Yes, he asked me to stop. No, I didn't do it just for him."

"Was your tobacco sacrifice sufficient to keep the two of you together?"

"Rhett Butler, no gentleman asks a lady such questions."

"Frankly, my dear..." He let his voice trail off. The effort to hide a smile was nearly too much for him now. Ethan gave her a studious frown, then watched something dark and painful flicker in her expression. She looked up, her eyes stoical, and he felt a rush of sympathy that neared the intensity from earlier, at the memorial. There was some sad story connected to the mysterious man friend, he assumed.

Tara absorbed the softening in his eyes and her breath pulled short. No. She couldn't fall into this muddle of sentiment, not with this disturbing man at hand to wreak havoc. He was fascinating, but he was also immoral, by her standards. Any man who headed a tobacco company had to have an underdeveloped conscience. Her mouth flattened in grim resistance, then she asked, "Why is Logan Tobacco diversifying? Are you planning to move away from the tobacco industry eventually?"

Now it was Ethan's turn to catch his breath. His eyes narrowed, and he leaned forward. She had a sudden mental image of angry energy crackling in sparks around him.

"Who told you that?" he demanded, his voice low and fierce. "Who the hell has been feeding you information?"

"What makes you think that I have an infor—"

"Don't," he interrupted, holding up one hand. "Don't bother to deny it. Don't waste my time. I know, the president of the company knows, and the board of directors knows that somebody in the upper ranks is supplying you with this confidential material."

"All right." Tara exhaled slowly and sat back, watching him, thinking about her next words. The waiter returned with their drinks. She took a minute to pour the brandy into her coffee and raise it to her lips for a generous sip. Ethan never moved. Finally, cautiously, she returned her gaze to his.

"I still can't tell you who it is," she said firmly.

"Tell me this." His voice was razor sharp. "What is this person's motive? Do you know?"

"This person..." She paused, assessing him, afraid of saying the wrong thing, saying anything that his sharp ears might trace to her informant. It would be an interesting war, she thought, if word ever got out that the informant was Maggie Logan, the last Logan of the dynasty that had begun Logan Tobacco 130 years ago in Kentucky. "This person has strong reservations about the morality of selling tobacco products. This person wants Logan Tobacco to get out of the business altogether."

A glimmer of victory shone in Ethan's eyes. He smiled thinly. "It's Maggie Logan."

Tara didn't move, didn't flinch. She held her coffee cup to her lips and gazed at him over the rim, while inside she felt sick. You fool! she told herself. You gave Maggie away! The first rule of reporting was to inspire complete trust from your sources. Steady, steady, she warned. Bluff him. She hadn't given him anything condemning. He was bluffing her.

She set her coffee down, making certain that her hand didn't tremble, then she smiled cordially and shook her head. "It won't work. You can't spew names at me and look for a shocked reaction. Don't be ridiculous."

Ethan grasped her wrist suddenly—not in a painful grip but a firm one. "Tell her," he said, his words falling like icicles, "that if she complicates anything I'm trying to do, I'll stir up more trouble than she's ever seen in her life. I can get her voted off the board if I have to."

Tara gazed directly into his eyes, seeing the ruthless confidence of a lion stalking a helpless prey. "It's not Maggie Logan," she insisted. "But answer my question. Is Logan diversifying?"

His eyes flickered down to her pad. "Off the record?"

"Yes."

"How do I know I can trust you?"

"You can, and you know it." She looked at him steadily, with the same confidence he displayed. "You may not like me, Mr. Boone, but you respect my work, I think. I'm a professional. Besides, what would it hurt for the world to know that Logan Tobacco is getting out of the tobacco business?"

"We're not getting out of the tobacco business. I never said that. Don't fish for information that way." He let go of her wrist and straightened slightly. "We're diversifying. That's all I can tell you. It's nothing exciting, nothing any other major corporation wouldn't do at this point in its corporate life."

"Look," Tara said quietly. "I'm not interested in the business aspects of Logan. I'm after your medical experts. But I would like to know how you can sleep at night when you're selling a product that's causing death and disease."

"Extremely well," he growled. Looking disgusted, Ethan took the shot glass of brandy and downed it in one gulp. The only sign of discomfort he allowed afterward was a slight tensing of his mouth, enough to momentarily deepen the lines etched there. Ethan looked at her coldly. It hurt like hell to know that she thought so badly of him when he was innocent of everything but being loyal to Logan. And he had good reasons for that loyalty.

"Don't you have any moral convictions?" she asked tautly, her face full of distaste.

Defeat settled in him and made him reckless. "Not by your standards. You'll be happy to know that before I came to work for Logan, I was CEO at Allied Foods. We made vending-machine food, lots of starchy, salty, sugary food full of preservatives. So I'm used to working in a despicable industry. In fact, I like being a monster. I love it when lab rats go belly-up from eating cookies and smoking cigarettes."

"You have a lovely sense of humor, Mr. Boone," she said sardonically. "But I think I've had enough of it."

"Why are you in Washington?" he demanded. "To cover the congressional hearings?"

"No. As I've already indicated, neither the business nor the politics of advertising bans interest me. I only get involved when medical experts start making claims and pointing to research statistics." She stood and gathered her coat off the booth's wall beside him, stepping close to him as she did so. "I'm the keynote speaker at a national conference of medical writers."

"Please, invoke my name in a curse during your speech," he said dryly. "I want you to be a success."

Tara stood still, her coat held against her stomach as she looked down at him. He was no more profit-motivated than the average business type, but she wanted him to be different. He'd captured her imagination at the monument. He'd brought life to her withered emotions with his simple kindness and shared grief. He had seemed tremendously special. She wanted him to be special.

Ethan stood also. He looked down into her green eyes and found himself drowning. They were so sad and distraught that every ugly emotion inside him drained away and was replaced with the knowledge that he was dying to be anything but her enemy.

"Don't leave," he said quickly. "Let's calm down and start over."

"No." She had to escape before she lost herself—a piece of her stupid, lonely soul—to him. *Damn him.* "I have a dinner date with friends. Here, let me give you some money..."

She reached for her purse, but he swept it off the table and into his hand. Ethan tucked both her pad and the tape recorder away, then snapped the purse shut and presented it to her.

"No. We..." For one of the few times in his life, he fumbled for words. "We were friends, in the park today. For that reason, let me buy."

Tara's eyes filled with sudden tears. She took the purse distractedly, looking up at him, trying to analyze the look in his eyes. Was it regret?

"Thank you," she whispered raggedly. Tara leaned forward and upward to brush a light kiss across his cheek, her eyes closed, her senses tuned to capture everything about him. "For the park." He inhaled with a rough sound as she stepped back. "I'm sure we'll be talking again," she told him. "Arguing, at least."

Sheer determination knotted under his breastbone. Yes, by God, he'd make certain their paths crossed. "We will," he agreed. She nodded with an elegant little movement of her head, then walked away. He remained standing and watched her until she disappeared out the door.

Three

It was nice being the editor of the health and science section for one of the largest daily newspapers in the world, Tara thought sardonically. So prestigious. People treated her with such awe. On her first day back from Washington, Tara stood in her tenth-floor cubicle and ruefully surveyed her desk—what she could see of it. It was covered with crumpled coffee cups, empty candy wrappers and stacks of unopened mail. A half-dozen memos were stuck to the back of her swivel chair, and an overflowing ashtray sat atop her computer terminal. She was staring at that ashtray, thinking about tobacco and Ethan Boone, mostly Ethan Boone, when Missy Coleman rushed in.

"Who's been torturing my office?" Tara deadpanned to her staff writer.

The lanky blonde was already blushing. "Larry and I both used it. We couldn't concentrate out at our desks. We meant to clean up before you came back, boss. I'm really

sorry. Especially about Larry's butts. The ashtray, I mean."
Larry Martin, Tara's other staff writer, was the smoker.

Tara pulled the memos off her chair and glanced over
them while Missy flung trash into the wastebasket and re-
stacked mail. "Leave the ashtray," Tara joked. "I crave the
aroma of cold cigarettes."

"Must have been a tough trip, if your smoking demon is
after you," Missy noted.

"Interesting trip," Tara corrected. That was an under-
statement, she added to herself. "What's this? I'm supposed to see Dan as soon as I get in? It's urgent?"

"Oh. Oh, yeah. It's about Logan Tobacco. Go right now,
boss. I'll dig you out a work space in here."

Frowning, Tara dropped her purse in the drawer of a file
cabinet and hurried out. She crossed the huge newsroom
floor, working her way through a maze of desks and computer terminals toward the managing editor's office at the
other side. Dan Alson's door was open. As she walked in,
he looked up over his black reading glasses, ran a pudgy
hand through nonexistent hair and cleared his throat in a
boisterous way that made his garish bow tie jiggle.

"Logan Tobacco?" Tara asked, shutting his door and
taking a seat in an upholstered chair across from his desk.
"Something wrong?"

"Yeah," he grunted. Dan always grunted, and he tended
to communicate in choppy sentences the staff had secretly
labeled "word blasts." "Could be. Call came yesterday.
Threatened libel suit. Crazy people. No chance they'd win.
Got a court order, though, about your memos. Those
memos of yours are restricted, judge said. Hell of a thing.
Sorry."

Tara's mouth fell open. "I can't publish the memos
Maggie Logan gave me?"

"Not right now." He gave her a curious look. "You know
the CEO at Logan? Ethan Boone?"

Tara nodded grimly, concerned. "We met in Washington. I interviewed him, but it didn't come to much."

"Came to something. He says he wants to talk. To you. Only you. Harvey's fit to be tied. He's wanted to interview Boone for months."

Harvey Bergen was the *Constitution*'s business editor. Elegantly thin, arrogant, the ultimate yuppie, he always seemed to be on the verge of a temper tantrum. "Harvey can go interview Mr. Boone, then," Tara said quickly. "Mr. Boone is trying to manipulate me." She nodded to emphasize her words. "The man wants to take some sort of revenge on me, I think."

"Good," Dan grunted. "Means you're doing your job." Someone rapped loudly on the office door. "In!"

The door was flung back. Tara looked up to see Harvey stomp in, his tortoiseshell glasses swinging from one slender hand, his red power tie askew, his exquisitely styled black hair ruffled. He glared at her, which she was used to. She gazed up at him calmly.

"Your pinstripes are all a-rumple, Harvey," she noted. "Calm down. I didn't mean to steal Ethan Boone from you."

Harvey slammed himself into a chair next to her. "Do you know that he's one of the most prized interviews in the free business world? He's very reclusive. What did you do in Washington? Kiss him?"

Tara bit her lip and looked at the ceiling. She *had* kissed Ethan Boone, dammit. "A good reporter never reveals her techniques, Harvey. What can I do to lower your blood pressure?"

"Take a list of my questions when you go to see him. Use whatever mysterious allure you used before and get his answers for me. Tape them. I'll take the tapes and write the stories, of course. You wouldn't understand the topics well enough to do it yourself."

"Harvey, no matter how hard you try, you can't insult me. I find your business doo-dahs extremely boring, and I don't *want* to write the stories. You can just add my name to your byline. The larger point here is that I don't intend to go see Ethan Boone. He's pulling us around by our noses. He can't do that."

"Oh, yes he can," Dan said flatly. "Anything we get from him is an exclusive for the business section. We'll be quoted by everybody from *U.S. News and World Report* to *The Wall Street Journal*. Big. Really big. Get it. Set the appointment. Go."

"Go," Harvey echoed, drumming his fingers on one knee.

Tara stood up, her back stiff with anger. She was being coerced by her boss, by a supercilious co-worker and, worst of all, by Ethan Boone. "You want interviews?" she asked Dan and Harvey in a proud voice. "I'll have the man eating out of my hand." She stalked out of the office, wishing she believed those words.

Tara was already craning her head back as she stepped out of a taxi in front of the Logan building on Fifth Avenue. She couldn't deny her awe as she looked up at the dignified old skyscraper, with its Gothic overtones. Logan Tobacco was a corporate solar system, and she was about to throw herself into the sun at its center, she mused with annoyance.

Logan owned more than a dozen companies. The biggies among them were Allied Foods, Flaverco Brands, Pizzazz Cola, Lucas-Byers Brewing and Ogden Tobacco, which had been a competitor of Logan Tobacco's decades ago. Tara rubbed her aching neck and headed into the building. She crossed an opulent lobby filled with an abstract art exhibit and entered one in a row of ornate elevators. She pushed a button for the twentieth floor and quickly reviewed the instructions given her by Ethan Boone's administrative assis-

tant. She had to get off at the twentieth floor and tell the
security people who she was, and they would escort her to
the executive offices on the thirtieth floor.

"Where his majesty awaits," she muttered under her
breath, watching numbers click by on the elevator's panel.
"Your slave girl is being brought to you, sire."

Being a slave in this palace would be interesting, Tara
conceded fifteen minutes later as a guard guided her across
the lobby of the executive floor. It was a mix-and-match
palace of plush contemporary furniture, rich old woods and
lush plants. Secretaries, some male, most female, com-
prised a large peasant class, she noted. The guard introduced her to Ethan Boone's administrative assistant. Dora
Brown was a pretty, middle-aged woman with Bette Davis
brusqueness. She made a call on an intercom line, then es-
corted Tara to a set of hand-carved double doors. The
woman opened one of them and gestured gracefully inside.

"Mr. Boone is expecting you," she intoned.

Here's where I'm supposed to fall down and grovel for
mercy, Tara thought wryly. Her trembling knees were already prepared. She took a deep breath and entered the office. The door clicked shut behind her. Trapped. Trapped in
the sun with a provocative blond king, she thought. He rose
from behind a huge mahogany desk, his expression a mixture of polite welcome and businesslike aplomb. As he came
toward her he ran one big hand down the lapel of a flawless
black suit, a European cut with a tiny white pinstripe.

Tara nodded formally in greeting and wished the turmoil
inside her weren't so undeniably sensual. He was sex and
power and courtly charm, with humor and compassion
thrown in for extras. She felt sad suddenly. If only he were
head of some morally justifiable company. If only she
weren't a reporter. If only she weren't trying to be loyal to a
man who might be dead, a man she no longer loved but still
honored.

Her mood somber, Tara took the hand Ethan Boone held out. Their gazes met as they shook hands briefly. Even in the course of that quick contact he managed to touch the delicate inner side of her wrist with the tip of his forefinger, squeeze her hand in a slow, intimate way and tickle the back of it with his thumb. She knew she'd never forget that handshake.

"I'm certainly glad you came," he said in his cultured Southern drawl.

"I confess I don't want to be here." She looked up at him with quiet anger. "It's interesting to be so close to such power, though. Do you usually manipulate people to get their attention?"

"Only when I can't get it any other way."

Ethan stepped back and studied her for a moment. Her jewelry was as unpretentious and practical as before, and her hair was swept back in neat waves. She wore a tailored white suit, red blouse and red pumps and carried a small red purse and a leather briefcase. As before, he found her business-like and yet very sexy. Her face was strong, and at the moment her cheeks were deeply flushed with annoyance. He wondered if passion would color her complexion the same pretty shade of pink.

"Why do I feel as if I'm modeling lingerie for you?" she said drolly.

"I'm sorry. How inconsiderate of me to stare." He smiled and motioned toward the floor-to-ceiling windows that dominated one whole wall of his huge office. Tara's gaze went to a table there that was set with crystal and linen.

"I hope you haven't eaten lunch," he told her. "Come have a glass of wine. I know drinking on the job must be horribly unethical for a reporter." He paused, his eyes glinting with a trace of mischief. "But that'll make it so much easier for me to manipulate you. Please have a drink and then eat lunch with me, Ms. Ross."

"I'm not impressed by any of this, Mr. Boone." She looked out at him from under her brows. "Or perhaps I *am* impressed, but quite aware that you're a master hypnotist. I can drink your wine and eat your lunch with perfect calm and then go my merry way, unscathed."

"I'd never scathe you," he teased her lightly. "Come and sit down."

Tara let him guide her across the room. He pulled out a chair for her and she settled at the table. "Your weapons, if you please, Ms. Ross." He held out his hands for her purse and briefcase. Tara's head dropped in defeat and a tiny smile fought its way to her lips. She handed them over and watched him carry them to an overstuffed leather chair. He went to his telephone console and pushed a button.

"We're ready to begin," he told some anonymous lackey, probably his Bette Davis clone, Tara decided. Then he came back to the table and sat down. Her heart thudding rapidly, Tara clasped her hands on the edge of the pristine table and looked at him seriously.

"That libel suit is a joke," she said frankly. "Everything I've ever written about your medical experts is documented."

"I'm afraid you're right. But my court order was a grand move, wasn't it?" A smile curved one corner of his firm mouth.

"Terrific. So what do you want to discuss with me?"

"I thought if you got to know me a little, you'd listen to me with an open mind."

A white-coated waiter slipped quietly through a side door in the big office. He came to the table, bowed to her, then presented the wine to Ethan Boone for approval. After the waiter left, Boone held up his glass in a salute. "To understanding each other," he offered.

Tara returned the toast. "To professional respect."

"Ah, no. It's my party, and I prefer 'To understanding each other,'" he protested blithely.

Tara couldn't help herself. She laughed, amused and exasperated. "You're hopelessly domineering."

"That's a good quality in an executive."

"But not in a human being."

He looked at her for a moment, his blue eyes growing solemn. "You really think I'm disgusting, don't you?" he asked with sincere interest.

Abashed, Tara lowered her gaze down to the fine china in front of her. She could almost believe he was hurt, she thought with surprising regret. She looked up at him again. "I guess I'm disappointed, not disgusted."

He leaned forward, the wineglass looking very fragile and forgotten in his hand, a hand that was too rugged for the elegant surroundings, she thought. All of him looked too rugged for this setting.

"Why are you disappointed?" he asked. "That sounds much more personal than I thought you cared to be with me."

Tara lifted her chin and eyed him warily. "I know that you're considered a brilliant businessman. I hate to see so much talent go into protecting a company that doesn't deserve protecting."

"Some of that is a compliment. Thank you."

Tara sighed and took a sip of wine. "I'm not a fanatic, Mr. Boone. I'm a practical person who understands that business is business and profits are profits, and when there's a demand for a product, somebody's going to provide that product. I just wish tobacco use weren't so dangerous and that you were a little concerned about the consequences."

Ethan struggled for a moment to keep calm, so frustrated that he could barely sit still. Someday he'd be able to tell her the truth, but it wouldn't matter if he'd already lost her. Lost her. That's what this was all about, this meeting today. He couldn't let himself lose this independent, stubborn, cool, heart-stopping woman.

"I won't argue the merits of smoking with you," he said wearily. "But I will remind you that the tobacco industry is an economic necessity to thousands of people—farmers, distributors, workers in the production plants, et cetera. If we shut down the industry tomorrow, we'd ruin livelihoods and lives."

"I know. I appreciate that fact."

He looked startled. "You're amazingly compliant," he joked.

"I'm no fanatic, as I said." This conversation was dissolving into sweetness and light, she realized abruptly. Tara cleared her throat. "If you want to get your point across, then let me do a series of interviews with you."

He smiled quizzically, but she noted the immediate enthusiasm in his eyes. "On the business angle?" he began. "I thought you didn't—"

"I don't." She explained about Harvey Bergen and the business section. "Look, I understand that you never give interviews. And if you *do* want to do this series, you'll want Mr. Bergen, not me—"

"Oh, I want you," he interjected. "Definitely."

"Mr. Bergen is more qualified—"

"I want you," he repeated. "Only you."

Tara stopped, her heart in her throat, her body registering a heated response to his words and the obvious personal meaning underneath them. "Because you respect my writing?" she asked bluntly.

"Yes." He leaned back, his chin tucked, his eyes combining mischief and seduction in a way that made her mouth dry and her palms damp. "I'd be a fool not to take you seriously as a reporter. You're excellent."

"And?"

"And..." He shrugged. "You're excellent," he repeated. He arched one dark blond brow at her and tilted his head in a way that made him look very innocent. "Are you concerned about something else?"

Not going to give an inch, are you, Mr. Boone? Tara thought grimly. We both know what's going on here, don't we? "I'm doing these interviews under duress," she informed him. "You dangled a very tempting bone in front of my managing editor."

"I'll certainly make your servitude as pleasant as I can," Ethan Boone said in a quaint voice. "I'm so sorry."

Tara arched one brow at him. "The heck you are."

"It *will* be pleasant, Tara. By the way, that's a lovely name. Let's use first names from now on."

"No thank you, Mr. Boone."

He chuckled, set his glass down and rubbed his hands in a show of open glee. "Well! So you're at my beck and call! Terrific!"

"Now, wait a minute—"

"We'll go to Kentucky this afternoon."

"What?" Her wineglass rattled against the china as she put it down.

"To the Logan estate. On one of the Logan jets. Right after lunch."

"What has the Logan estate got to do with our business interviews?"

He sighed grandly. "You can't understand Logan Tobacco unless you understand its roots, can you?"

The waiter returned with the first course of lunch. "Right. Roots," Tara muttered under her breath. The waiter set their plates down.

"No, I believe it's asparagus salad." Ethan smiled. He was the victor in this skirmish, and they both knew it.

The Logan jet purred with power as it reached cruising altitude outside the New York area. The pilot's voice, polite and friendly, came over a speaker. "It's okay to move around the cabin now, sir." Tara stopped digging her fingers into the arms of her plush seat.

Across the aisle from her, Ethan Boone unfastened his lap belt. "Thanks, Mike," he answered. "How's the weather look?"

"We're probably going to run through some thunderstorms thirty minutes or so before we reach the estate, sir. It looks pretty turbulent on radar."

Tara gripped her seat arms again. Her stomach also tried to find something to cling to. Failing, it drew up in knots.

"Tara?"

She swiveled her head to find Ethan Boone gazing at her with concern.

"You're pale. Are you all right?"

"Fine. Fine." She straightened quickly, unsnapped her belt and reached for her briefcase, which was under the seat. "Now. I'd like to get started on this first round of questions from Mr. Bergen, if you're ready."

"Fine. Fine," he mimicked her gently, getting up. His tall, powerful body filled the aisle, and his head was only a few inches away from the ceiling. His pants leg brushed her arm, and she pretended not to notice. Tara opened her briefcase and removed pad, pen and tape recorder.

"How about something to drink?" he asked.

"No more wine, please."

"We're being very professional, I know." He bent over her and casually propped one arm on the backrest of the seat in front of hers. The hand of his other arm rested on the backrest of her seat. Tara looked up and was startled to find Ethan Boone so close, so...everywhere...above her. His cologne was light, some expensive scent, she was certain. Tara inhaled its compelling essence and felt her stomach relax a little.

"Are you sure you're all right?" he asked again. "You look distracted."

"It's the company."

"Why, that's sweet." He smiled.

"Logan," she hurried to say. "I'm thinking about Logan Tobacco. That sort of company."

"Such unwarranted defensiveness!" He was still smiling. "Now, back to the question at hand. Since you insist on propriety, I'll get you something besides alcohol. Mineral water, juice, a soft drink—"

"What kind?" she asked slyly. "Pizzazz Cola, I bet."

He gave her a jaunty look. "Of course. It's corporate policy to stock the jets only with our brands."

"May I have a diet, decaffeinated Pizzazz Cola, then?"

"Only the best for you."

She watched him surreptitiously as he went behind a bar in one end of the small jet. He removed his jacket and vest, revealing a beautiful, oyster-white shirt as he turned to face her. His black silk tie was a striking accent down the front of a broad chest that had undoubtedly been honed in New York's most exclusive gyms. He slipped a gold pocket watch from his vest and laid it aside.

"Would you rather sit at the conference table up here or stay in your seat?" he asked.

Tara studied the elegant teakwood table. Its upholstered chairs looked very comfortable. She frowned; they didn't have seat belts. "I'd prefer to stay here, if you don't mind," she answered.

"No problem." By the time he returned with a crystal glass full of ice and cola, she had all her materials arranged on her briefcase and was ready for the interview. He sat down across from her, sipping a glass of mineral water with a slice of lime in it.

"Don't you drink Pizzazz Cola?" she asked.

"Hmm." She could tell that he didn't, but he wasn't going to admit it.

Tara smiled knowingly and turned on the tape recorder. "I see."

"No comment."

She looked at Harvey's list of questions and frowned. "This isn't going to be easy. Some of these terms are Greek to me."

"I'll be gentle. The first time is always difficult." Tara arched one brow at him and got an arched brow in return. She shook her head in mock disgust at his innuendo. He chuckled. "Let's talk about first times," he prodded. "Tell me about the first time you saw New York."

"I went there from a small daily paper in Nebraska. New York scared the hell out of me."

"Oh, a farm girl, eh?"

"Suburban Omaha."

"Family still there?"

"Uh-huh. My mother teaches nursing at the university. I have two married sisters."

"Older?"

"Younger. I'm the family's resident old-maid career woman."

"Hmm. By choice? A maid? Really?"

Tara turned quickly back to her papers and tape recorder. "First question, Mr. Boone. It concerns your management style." He groaned in defeat and leaned back in his seat, smiling.

"I'm reputed to be a persuasive, charismatic man," he quipped. "But I think you've shot that image down nicely."

Tara made a gleeful sound. "Thank you. Now..."

Nearly an hour passed in relative peace. She asked questions and he answered them. Harvey's questions weren't the kind that put him on the defensive, Tara decided. They were tough and complicated, but they focused on safe subjects. His management style. Corporate organization. His background with the conglomerate. That part intrigued her deeply.

"You've worked for Logan since you were fourteen years old?" she asked, amazed.

· He nodded. "Started at the Allied Foods plant in Kentucky, sweeping floors and cleaning machinery. Killihan Logan, the old man—that's an affectionate reference, I assure you—took a liking to me. He didn't have any grandsons, and he was a tough old hellion who wasn't easy to tolerate. But I understood him, and he understood me—" the jet bounced and swayed "—so he told me that I had potential, and that—Tara?"

Tara had turned to stare at the churning clouds outside her window. They closed around the jet like a dense, dark fog. The engines roared with sudden strain. Swallowing hard, she twisted back to face Ethan Boone. "I'm . . . sorry. Go ahead, Mr. Boone."

The pilot's voice came over the intercom. "It's time to put on the seat belts again, sir. We're moving into those storms I mentioned. Don't worry, but this ride may be a roller coaster until we land."

"Thanks, Mike," Ethan answered with absolute calm. Tara thought he was actually about to stifle a yawn. She had never felt less like yawning in her life. He took their glasses and put them away. When he came back, he pointed to her unfastened seat belt. "Better connect that again."

Tara smiled weakly. He didn't have to urge her to buckle up. She turned her tape recorder off, set it and the briefcase in the window seat to her left and hurried to fasten her belt, her fingers trembling violently. Suddenly Ethan Boone's large, capable hands were resting atop hers, pushing them out of the way.

Tara looked up in amazement. He bent down, keeping his attention on the belt, but once it was fastened, he looked directly into her eyes. There was quiet compassion in his face. "You can't hide it," he murmured. "It's okay."

Tara leaned her head against the seat and looked at him wearily while he sat down and buckled his own belt. "I only lose my cool when I have to fly through storms," she assured him. "I'm reasonably relaxed on a normal airplane flight."

He leaned sideways in his seat so that he could face her. "Any reason for your fear? Your father...he was killed flying for the military, right?"

"No, that has nothing to do with my phobia. I'm just highly sensitive to the notion that airplanes sometimes fall down. It's really not a big problem."

The jet lurched again, and she sank her fingers convulsively into the seat arms.

"Hey," Ethan said gently. "We're going to be fine. Believe me."

Tara took a shallow breath and nodded. "If I were going to believe anybody in the world, it would be you."

"Oh?" He smiled.

"You radiate command. No jet would dare crash with you on board."

He laughed. The jet pitched suddenly. Tara closed her eyes and shuddered. "Oh, I hate this," she whispered. "I feel like a real wimp."

"Ssssh." She opened her eyes in shock as she heard him getting up.

"Don't!" she urged. "Sit down!"

"I'm going to get you a shot of bourbon."

"Oh...well...that's probably a good idea."

"Put your things away."

Tara fumbled with her briefcase and had it secured under the seat by the time he returned. He carried a small plastic cup with dark liquid in the bottom. He guided her shaking hand around the cup. "Shoot it," he ordered.

"Good heavens." She grimaced and put the cup to her lips, then tossed the contents down her throat. "Ew! Blah! That's awful!"

"I'm so glad that Logan doesn't own a brand of bourbon," he intoned wryly. "I'd be insulted."

Tara looked up at him with wistful regard. "Sorry." The bourbon hit her stomach then, and she blinked slowly.

"Ah, the owl look has already come over those beautiful green eyes. Feel better?" He braced himself as the jet bounced again.

Tara nodded without enthusiasm. "I'm going to hate myself later for this, but—" she squinted up at him in wretched embarrassment "—does this jet's brand-name booty include any Laramie cigarettes?"

He stared at her for a long moment, disbelief showing in his eyes. "Yes. But I'm not going to let you—"

"Please. Just one."

"No, Tara. You're not serious."

"I'm a dedicated nonsmoker now, I really am."

"One cigarette leads to another...."

"Oh, no, it won't. I've done this before, on airplanes. It's harmless." She gave him her most hopeful look, while deep down she recognized the bizarreness of the situation. An avid reformer was pleading for a cigarette from a cigarette king, and he didn't want to give her one.

Ethan sighed. "Just one." The jet swayed and dipped as he went back to the front and opened a cabinet. He returned and motioned at her seat belt. "Move over. We'll share."

Tara hurriedly complied, moving into the window seat and refastening her belt. He sat down beside her and fastened his. Then he held up a cigarette and a small gold lighter.

"Unfiltered," Tara said in awe. "Bless your heart."

She watched his profile as he placed the cigarette between his lips. It gave him a whole different look, street-smart and tough. He cupped his hands around the end of it and flicked the lighter. "You must have smoked cigarettes once upon a time," she noted. "You're a natural."

He smiled and took it from his mouth. "I smoked a few in my younger years." He handed the cigarette to her, his fingers brushing hers. The plane veered sharply to one side.

Her eyes shut, Tara jabbed the Laramie between her lips and took a long drag. "Oh, it's wonderful," she said weakly. When she opened her eyes again, Ethan Boone was gazing at the contours of her mouth. Feeling reckless from the bourbon, she placed the cigarette back between her lips. Slowly, she inhaled. Looking at him squinty-eyed, she pursed her mouth and blew smoke in a long, graceful stream straight up in the air, where it was whisked away by the jet's air-conditioning system.

"You're marvelous at that," he said hoarsely.

"I can blow smoke rings, as well. Watch this, Ethan."

She gave him a brief demonstration, but in the midst of it she realized that she'd just called him by his first name. Tara quickly fanned the smoke rings away and handed him the cigarette. "I'm done," she said crisply. "Thank you, Mr. Boone."

"Smoke some more," he teased her. "It makes you a different person."

She looked away, smiling pensively. He took one more drag on the cigarette and ground it out in the ashtray on the arm of his seat. Tara sighed. "It was nice while it lasted."

Suddenly the jet leaped as if a giant hand had just swatted it from underneath. Tara hugged herself and shut her eyes tightly. When Ethan Boone pried one of her hands out and held it, she gave him a grateful look. He leaned back in his seat and turned his face close to hers. "Talk," he commanded. "Tell me about yourself."

Tara inhaled sharply, nodded and began. For fifteen minutes she talked nonstop, her eyes directly on his, as if his gaze were a lifeline. He listened without ever looking away, and he rubbed small, soothing circles on her hand. She talked about her family, about the Manhattan condominium she'd sweated to buy, about her early jobs working for small newspapers and medical newsletters. Finally they heard the pilot's voice.

"Sir, we're making our final approach to the estate airfield. It's going to be rough, so hold on. We'll be down in about five minutes."

"Oh, I wish he hadn't put it that way," Tara joked lamely.

Ethan Boone laughed. "You're too sharp for your own good."

"I know."

"I think it's wonderful."

They traded a silent look that brimmed with unexpected affection, and abruptly he let go of her hand and slipped his arms around her. It seemed the most natural thing in the world. She leaned against him, cradled in the crook of his shoulder, her teeth chattering from nerves.

"Awful," she managed. "I-I'm a-a w-wimp."

He guided her head into the curve of his neck. "You're terrific," he whispered. "For a wimp."

She chuckled and got her teeth under control. "I owe you one for putting up with me."

"Call me Ethan instead of Mr. Boone and we'll be even."

"Good enough."

"Say it."

"You domineering . . . *Ethan*. Ethan."

He pulled her tighter to him and turned his face so that his cheek was against her temple.

"Ethan," she said again more softly.

His voice was a low, inviting rumble. "See? Practice makes perfect."

The jet bumped repeatedly on pockets of air. Tara wound her fingers into Ethan's shirtfront. "I'll buy you a new one if I rip this," she quipped.

"I wouldn't mind you tearing my shirt off," he murmured. He stroked her shoulders and back. "Another minute, and we'll be on the ground."

When she made a small sound of distress as the jet wobbled from side to side, he brought his hands up slowly, sank his fingers into her hair and eased her head back so that their mouths were a bare inch apart.

"There's only one thing that might take your mind off your fear," he told her.

And then his lips closed over hers, coaxing, firm and insistent. Tara gasped in surprise. He was right; it was a very effective distraction. His tongue slid inside her parted lips and tested her willingness for a deeper intimacy. Tara groaned softly and opened her mouth farther, then met his tongue with her own.

His lips were mobile and skilled as they captured her mouth again and again. She knew vaguely that she was kissing him back, running her tongue over his lower lip, tugging gently at one corner of his mouth, kissing his chin and cheek before offering herself again for the warm, irresistible invasion of his tongue.

He swirled it around her own, then drew back to plant a series of light kisses on her face. "You're gorgeous," he whispered. "Fantastic." He bent his head and gently nudged hers to one side so that he could kiss her throat. He sucked gently on a spot there, then moved up to her ear and nibbled the lobe. "Feel better?"

"Yes. Oh, yes," she moaned. "Oh, Ethan. This is so... Don't stop...."

"Well, how did you like that landing, sir?" The pilot's voice was a booming interruption over the intercom. Tara jerked back and looked up at Ethan's flushed face and hooded eyes. He was breathing roughly, and she realized that she was, too. And not from fear.

"What landing?" she whispered. "We're on the ground?" She paused, her eyes wide with speculation. "We're on the ground, Ethan!"

Ethan shook his head groggily and cleared his throat. "That was a *damned* good landing, Mike." His gaze held hers with mesmerizing invitation, and his voice dropped to a throaty murmur as he said, "The best ever."

Four

The Logan estate was named Dunverary, after the castle of a mythical Scottish king, Ethan explained as they walked slowly through sumptuous, darkly paneled halls lined with the kind of art and antiques that only a fortune could buy. Tara clasped her hands behind her back and listened distractedly while a churning part of her mind tried to clarify how she felt about the disturbing incident on the jet.

A Logan employee had whisked them through the manicured estate grounds in a black Mercedes sedan, so there had been no private moment in which she could confront Ethan. She'd gazed blankly at the majestic baronial mansion that formed the centerpiece of Dunverary's main grounds. She'd nodded with vague politeness to Joshua, the casually elegant overseer who greeted them at the mansion's massive doors. Even now, thirty minutes after Ethan's kiss, she still felt flushed and upset.

"...so Dunverary was completed in 1879," Ethan said, "by Tavis Logan. He was the first Logan born in America.

He went out to the California goldfields as a young man and struck it rich. Tavis was a hell-raiser, from what I've been told. He didn't care for convention, and he proved that later by marrying Katacha Gallatin, who was part Cherokee. Their portraits are in the library here. They were quite a pair. One of their children was Killihan Logan's grandfather.''

"A very romantic story," Tara said drolly. As they entered a huge garden room filled with greenery and sunlight, she felt Ethan's eyes on her. She glanced at him. He gave her an enigmatic smile.

"I'm a very romantic person," he offered, his tone soft. "Especially in airplanes."

"Ah. I knew my crime would eventually come back to haunt me."

A maid appeared from somewhere, bearing a silver tea service and croissants on an ornate tray. "Nice to see you again, Mr. Boone," she said pleasantly, then deposited the tray on a white wrought-iron table. "Thank you for the flowers you sent to my mother. She's much better."

Tara made a mental note of his thoughtful gesture.

"Glad to hear it. Nice to see you, Anne." After she left, Ethan motioned to a long settee near the table. "Please."

Tara sat down, frowning. He fixed her a cup of tea, then offered a croissant stuffed with cream cheese and dates. She took the tea but shook her head at the food. "I'm not here to be pampered. I'm here to work."

"You need to be pampered. You have an austere look about you. I bet you don't treat yourself to many luxuries."

"Such as letting my interview kiss me? That was an unethical and unprofessional ploy."

"Unethical?" Smiling slightly, Ethan shook his head. He stood by the settee, looking down at her and ignoring the ludicrously delicate teacup in his hand. With the pin-striped jacket back in place on his broad shoulders, he presented a devastating image of class and confidence.

"I know about McGee Webster," he said suddenly.

Tara's fingers tightened around her cup in shock. She scrutinized Ethan for a moment. His expression was now carefully neutral. He was so damned cool, wasn't he? she thought angrily. "I see. You just told your lackeys to do a background check on Tara Ross and—voilà—you have it. Do you investigate the personal life of every reporter who interviews you?"

"I've only given a couple of interviews since I became CEO at Logan."

"I know. And this one is going to be much more in-depth than those were. Why do you give so few interviews, Ethan?"

"Reporters think they have to analyze me as well as Logan Tobacco. I don't want my private life scrutinized by the public. It isn't relevant."

"You have something to hide?" Tara asked carefully.

He gave her a rebuking look. "My private life isn't relevant," he repeated.

"All right, agreed. Then why is *my* private life relevant to these interviews?"

Ethan smiled. "I just find it interesting."

Tara shook her head in defeat. "Irrelevant."

"Irrelevant to business concerns, perhaps."

She gazed at him silently, feeling flattered and anxious at the same time. There was something unnerving about a man who would go to such trouble to find out so much about her. "Exactly what have you learned?" Tara asked in a small voice.

"McGee Webster, veteran cameraman for National Network News," he recited calmly, "went to Lebanon on assignment two years ago. He disappeared shortly thereafter, and the Shiite Muslims claimed responsibility for kidnapping him. He hasn't been heard from since." Ethan paused, and gentleness crept into his voice. "The State Department is reasonably certain that his kidnappers killed him."

Tara nodded grimly. "But that's based only on rumors. There's no proof." She stared down at her cup. "And?"

"And...during the five years before he left for Lebanon, he and you were..."

"Yes." *Lovers.* She was reluctant to hear Ethan use the words. She didn't feel embarrassed but simply thought that the subject was too intimate and provocative to discuss with a man who had recently torn all her defenses apart.

"And?" he prompted her.

"I'm waiting for him to come back."

He mused over that vague comment for a second. "The word I received was that your relationship was nearly over when he left."

Tara stood, trembling with surprise and anger. Ethan Boone's sources were amazingly accurate. She set her cup down and walked to a window, where she stood with her back to him, staring out at a panorama of fine lawns and regimented flower gardens. She had talked McGee into taking the Lebanon assignment, because the separation would make their breakup easier. Her unwavering principles would never let her forget that she was partially responsible for what had happened to him.

There had once been a great deal of happiness between her and McGee, though they had been a mismatched couple from the start, and now—McGee was still alive. She didn't care what the State Department said. Alive, and perhaps clinging to those happy memories like a lifeline.

"Do you still love McGee Webster?" Ethan asked.

Tara kept her face turned away from his shrewd gaze. She owed McGee her loyalty. It was all she could give him, in apology. And there was only one way to sidetrack Ethan's unerring attention.

"My personal feelings are personal," she said softly.

Silence settled in the large room, and she felt goose bumps on her spine as Ethan's footsteps sounded on the cool white slate. He stopped beside her, and Tara looked up at him with a rigidly guarded expression. Sunlight glinted invitingly on his thick blond hair. His eyes were troubled and searching as they locked on hers. "I suspect that you're evading the answer because you don't love him anymore but you'd feel guilty admitting it," he noted smoothly.

Tara sighed in dismay and quickly focused on the flowers outside rather than his intuitive gaze. "Your honor, prosecution is badgering the defendant," she quipped to an invisible judge. Tara cleared her throat roughly. "None of this should concern you, Ethan. It has nothing to do with our professional relationship."

"Everything about you is of concern to me. I'm not talking about our *professional* relationship. Just our relationship, period."

She shook her head, but dully acknowledged that his words rearranged her emotions into a jumble of ache and need. She and Ethan were drawn to each other in ways they didn't yet understand, and no amount of rational skepticism would erase the attraction. At the veteran's memorial they had connected immediately, and the give and take of emotions was as intense now as then. It was almost as if she'd known a secret, silent language all her life and had finally found the one person who could share it.

A desperate need for resistance made her whirl toward him suddenly, her eyes narrowed. "You run a tobacco company. My personal principles will never let me forget that, regardless of anything else. And my professional principles won't let me think of you as anything but an interview."

His eyes flickered with a bitterness that puzzled her. "Principles," he repeated sardonically. "Of which I have none, you suspect."

"You have principles. Just not the same as mine."

"A generous, if patronizing, assessment. You might come to think better of me if you'd give your staunch idealism a rest."

Her strange panic grew, and she raised her hands in supplication. But before she could say anything, he grasped them tightly.

"Enough," he told her. He seemed to know that she was on the verge of canceling their interviews without regard for the consequences at the newspaper. "Realize," he added in a lower voice, "that my board of directors wouldn't exactly *approve* if they knew I'd taken a personal interest in a writer who's caused the company so much trouble. So...you and I are in the same moral dilemma."

He gave her a mildly rebuking look. "Pardon me. I forget that I *have* no morals. But it's a dilemma nonetheless." He let go of her hands and stepped back, withdrawing into a polite and impersonal attitude. "So I volunteer to put this relationship back on strictly professional grounds."

She studied him with shrewd eyes, then slowly exhaled in relief. "I suspect that you're bluffing," she noted drolly. "But thank you." He nodded, humor crinkling his eyes. Oh, yes, we both know what game we're playing, don't we? Tara asked silently.

"What size blue jeans do you wear?" he asked.

She looked at him askance. He was changing course in midstream, she thought nervously. And she didn't know which way to paddle. "Pray tell, why?"

"We keep a collection of clothes upstairs, for guests. Anne will help you find something appropriate."

"Pray tell, why? I ask again."

He smiled patiently. "We're about to go horseback riding."

"I never mix business with large, unpredictable animals."

"You lead a dull life, then." Smiling, he took her arm and guided her toward the hallway.

Ethan sat astride the leggy gray gelding with a panache that drew covert, admiring looks from her. His jeans fit with a disarming degree of snugness. They were faded in a way that told her he wore jeans often, and that intrigued her. In his scuffed Western boots and white polo shirt, he could have posed for an urban version of Logan's trademark, Laramie Man. As her fat chestnut gelding stepped lazily along beside Ethan's horse, Tara glanced down at her borrowed attire. The short-sleeved plaid shirt and crisp dark jeans fit amazingly well, and even the dove-gray boots seemed made to order.

"My sisters and I had horses when we were growing up," she remarked. "But it's been years since I've ridden."

"You're doing fine."

"You ride as if you grew up on a ranch."

"The old man insisted that I take riding lessons here. He considered horsemanship a social requirement."

"Killihan Logan must have really treated you like a member of the family."

"Hmm. I was a substitute grandson." Ethan paused, then added pensively. "He was good to me. And I'm loyal to the people who are good to me."

She pondered that remark, wondering why it had sounded almost regretful.

The horses followed a winding trail through a field of lush grass. The central Kentucky landscape was as beautiful as she'd always heard. Gently rolling hills sloped into shallow valleys aproned in thick forests. "When does the grass turn blue?" Tara asked.

"About the middle of June. It blooms then." He arched one brow at her. "You should come back and see it."

"Oh, the interviews will be finished long before that," she answered drolly. He smiled.

They entered a virgin hardwood forest on the other side of the field and Tara craned her head back to gaze up at the huge trees. "How many acres does Dunverary encompass?"

"Three thousand, give or take a dozen."

"Just your average old Kentucky home, then."

He laughed, the sound rich and inviting. Shadows slid over them, and the forest muffled the thud of the horses' hooves into a low, pleasant rhythm.

"So," she said lightly, "where is the Boone family castle? Nearby, I assume."

"A few miles from here. Close to the Allied Foods plant."

"Where you began your illustrious business career by sweeping floors."

His answer was a little taunting. "That's right. Back when I still had my principles and morals."

Tara's mouth thinned as she absorbed the light jab. "I'm certain you still do," she told him.

"No. I'm a fiendish tobacco merchant now. Tainted but successful."

She saw that this line of conversation could turn angry at the slightest push, so she quickly changed it. "And has there ever been a *Mrs.* Tainted-but-Successful?"

He tossed a wicked look her way. "No, but there *have* been quite a few applications for the position. I'm always on the lookout for the perfect candidate."

"Executive wife, model A-one," Tara intoned gravely. "*Playboy* body, Miss America manners. She runs the house superbly, never slurps her soup at important business dinners, volunteers for all the correct charity events and makes certain the requisite two-point-five executive children always behave commendably."

"How have I managed without her all these years!"

"Beats me."

"Could it be that she's not my type?"

"Hmm. An interesting but unlikely premise."

They continued the light banter as they rode deeper into the woods. Fifteen minutes later they rounded a curve in the trail and came to a broad silver stream. A burly dark-haired man with a beard shadow straightened ominously beside it. Tara widened her eyes in alarm as she noted the pistol holstered against the leg of his dirty overalls. He wore no shirt, and his bare arms were fleshy but muscled. He held a fishing rod in one hand. She was dimly aware that Ethan angled his horse slightly in front of hers, as if shielding her from the sly grin that slid across the man's face.

"How are ya, Ethan?" he drawled in a thick accent. Puzzled by that lazy familiarity, Tara glanced at Ethan's face and saw that his jaw was clenched.

"Haven't seen you in a while, Carl."

"Just got out. Good behavior. Thought I'd fish a little." The grin simmered beneath calm, untrustworthy eyes. "You're lookin' good, as usual. Visitin' from New York?"

"Just down for the day." Tara found Ethan's gaze on her. "Why don't you ride ahead?" he instructed her in a polite tone that was underscored with tension. "I'll catch up with you in a minute."

"All right." Bewildered, she guided her horse across the stream and up the trail on the opposite side. Tara twisted in the saddle to give Ethan a final look. She caught the man, Carl, staring at the athletic curve of her rump with unabashed interest. She watched Ethan's expression harden even more as he noted that slow survey. He caught her eye and urged her on with a slight movement of his head. She nudged her mount into a faster walk and quickly left the stream behind a new bend in the trail.

The exchange of masculine animosity had been fascinating, she mused. She rode for several minutes, her brow furrowed, then stopped the horse and waited. The gray loped gracefully into sight. Ethan reined it to a halt beside her. His eyes and taut body posture radiated tension.

"Sorry about that," he told her. They rode on, and silence stretched between them.

"You have interesting friends," Tara ventured.

He studied her for a moment, as if mulling over a decision. "That was no friend," he said finally. "That was my second cousin."

She sat back in her saddle and eyed him with what she hoped was a nonchalant look. Ethan almost smiled.

"Thank you for trying not to appear shocked," he said wryly.

Tara sighed in defeat. "It's hopeless. Your second *cousin*?"

"Hmm. I don't want you to think he's typical of the people here. The South isn't made up of extras from the cast of *Deliverance*."

"I know that," she answered gently.

He gave her a grateful look, but his face remained grim. "However, he's a pretty typical representation of my family."

Astonished, she finally managed to say, "Why is he on the grounds of Dunverary?"

"Locals are allowed to fish and hunt here, with permission." He paused. "Carl just got out of prison. He and my other cousins have a penchant for *borrowing* other people's trucks." Ethan smiled thinly. "It's sort of a family business."

"My family has a side like that," she assured him. Inside, she was still stunned. Ethan and his second cousin were at opposite ends of the evolutionary scale. "Great-uncle Cameron served time for fraud. He sold nonexistent mobile-home lots."

Ethan smiled at her solemn confession. Then the smile faded and he faced forward, a muscle working in his jaw. "Everything I just told you is off the record," he said. "And everything I'm about to tell you, too."

She inhaled slowly. "All right."

"If it weren't for Killihan Logan, I'd probably be stealing trucks, too. Or worse. When he caught me trying to swipe a television set from Dunverary, I was well on my way to becoming a criminal."

"But . . . you were only fourteen!"

"In my family," Ethan answered drolly, "we started young."

"What did he do?"

"He said, 'Boy, I can turn you over to the sheriff or you can go to work for me.' I wasn't fond of either alternative, but I chose work."

"And you reformed."

"Only because Killihan Logan threatened to kill me if I didn't. If you'd known the old man, you'd understand why that threat put the fear of God into a juvenile delinquent."

"But he obviously saw that you were smart and had potential. That's why he went to the trouble." She paused, thinking. "So he became your mentor?"

"That's right. Later he paid my way to college, with the understanding that I'd come back here and work for him."

"What did your parents think of that?"

"My mother died when I was seven, and my father didn't give a damn what I or my brothers did."

"One brother died in . . . Vietnam. I remember your telling me you had another brother."

"Younger than me. Noah. I made sure he didn't end up in trouble, too. I helped him through college, and now he's got a big farm a few hours west of here. I'm very proud of him." He paused, arching a brow at her. "He grows tobacco, among other things."

"Aha. I see."

"So that's my background."

"Tell me more about your family—"

"No. I just wanted you to know the basics."

Tara felt the heat of an angry blush begin easing up her neck. "We're off the record, you recall. You can trust me." She hesitated, frowning. "Is your background one reason that you stay away from the press? You don't want questions—"

"From gossip mongers—that's right."

"Which includes me, I suppose."

He studied her in annoyed silence, eyes narrowed. "It's nothing personal."

"It's very damned personal. I'm not interviewing you for *The National Enquirer*."

"Consider yourself flattered, Tara. I don't tell many people about my background."

"But it's fascinating and inspirational—"

"And private. You don't need to know any more."

She faced forward, her chest tight with an odd feeling. After a second's analysis, she realized that she was wounded because he had shut her out. *That's a personal reaction, not a professional one,* she told herself harshly. *Get rid of it.*

"When we return to the house, I'd like to change clothes and go on with the interview," she said coolly.

"We'll be flying back to New York in a couple of hours. You can finish the interview on the jet."

"You always call the shots," she retorted. "Whatever you say, sir."

"You're beautiful when you're angry," he quipped.

"I'm not angry. I'm disappointed. I had begun to think that under that power-broker exterior I might find a human being."

"You're not concerned with human beings. You're concerned with issues and idealism."

"Let's change the subject."

"Let's avoid the facts." He smiled triumphantly, then squinted at the sky. "Lovely weather for this time of year, don't you think?"

The stables at Dunverary were larger and better kept than most homes, Tara noted as she led her horse down a cool brick corridor. Ahead of her, Ethan sent the gray into a luxurious stall and began to unsaddle him. He directed her toward one beside it.

"The stable manager must be out on an errand," he told her. "I'll pull the gear off your horse as soon as I finish with this one."

"I can do it myself." She led the chestnut into its stall and worked at the gear fastenings, her head down. Their earlier conversation still stung, no matter how much he tried to change her mood.

"Do you do *everything* for yourself?" he called.

"Yes. I'm one of those women who're described as *sturdy*."

"Athletic, tough—"

"I run an eight-minute mile and play a mean game of softball."

"A regular amazon." He appeared in the door to the stall and took the heavy Western saddle from her. She laid the bridle and blanket on top of it while she squinted up at him defensively.

"Able to take care of myself," she countered.

"Lonely," he replied, and left.

Tara stepped out of the stall, shut the door hard and glared at his broad back as he went into a tack room farther down the hallway. A mewing sound reached her ears, distracting her. She traced it to an empty stall and went inside, her boots sinking deep into rustling yellow straw.

"Kittens," she whispered happily when she found the nest in one corner. The mother cat, a fat calico, purred and stretched as Tara knelt beside her. She stroked one of the kittens with the tip of her forefinger. "Aren't you cute?" she murmured.

"I should have been a cat." She looked up quickly. Ethan walked across the stall and sat down on his boot heels. He scratched the mother cat under the chin. "Candy, you're a party girl," he told her wryly. "Not again."

"She's just doing what comes naturally."

"You approve?"

"In Candy's case I do."

"But not for yourself."

"I'm not calico." She gestured toward her dark hair. "Brunettes are very tame and proper."

"Even when they don't want to be," he countered.

She stood up, and he followed. They faced each other, sharing a gaze that was suddenly sensual and intense. The barn was quiet except for the small sounds made by the horses. The air was fragrant with a mixture of scents—hay, leather and the April flowers outside. The air promised fertility, Tara thought. She took a shallow breath and felt her pulse increase. This was the time of year for making babies.

She knew he was going to kiss her, and she shut her eyes as he leaned forward to do it. Trembling, she stood still and felt his mouth close slowly over hers. He clasped her shoulders, but she kept her hands by her sides in tight fists. She inhaled the arousing scent of his skin and body. His cologne had given way to light sweat and fresh air, and there was also a pleasant, musky aroma, a primitive male enticement.

His tongue separated her lips and teased her. With a little sigh of dismay, her body turning into a liquid traitor, she opened her mouth and twisted it slowly against his. He slid his hands up her shoulders, then down the front of her shirt. The backs of his strong, blunt fingers brushed over her breasts, then lingered, teasing where he knew nipples were hidden. Tara gasped as the peaks swelled to meet his expert touch, and he lightly circled the hard buttons with his fingertips.

She trembled harder, refusing to touch him but too overwhelmed to step back. He sensed her inner conflict and kissed her more intimately, nudging her with little movements of his jaw, his mouth mobile and tender. His fingertips roamed down her stomach, then flared over her hips. He trailed his fingers up and down her thighs until she shifted with involuntary pleasure, helpless.

Tara took a tentative step toward him, and his hands flattened on her sides. Pressing tightly, he slipped them around her and cupped her rump, rubbing small circles. The combined caress of soft denim and Ethan's firm grip made her whimper. She uncurled her fists and started to reach for him.

He let go of her and stepped back, his chest moving roughly, his eyes hooded with control. Tara gazed up at him in distress and anger. After a moment she believed that she could almost breathe again. "You proved your point," she whispered hoarsely.

He nodded. "Now that you know how I grew up, you understand. Anything I wanted badly, I'd just steal. I didn't care about wrong or right." His voice was throaty. "There's still a side of me that makes me reckless that way, Tara. I don't care if you're a risk to Logan. I don't care if you're trying to be loyal to a man who might be dead. I'm going to steal you, someday." He paused, and determination gleamed in his eyes. "Fair warning."

She raised one hand to her face, wondering if she looked the same, if she *was* the same or ever would be again. "Fair warning," she murmured.

Five

Maggie Logan never just walked into a room. She swept in and took command, designer suit shouting prestige, head up in regal splendor, strawberry-red hair piled high in the latest style. Tara eyed Killihan Logan's beautiful granddaughter with admiration as Maggie invaded the cramped back-street diner, adding glamour to the lives of the low-echelon office workers who gaped at her in amazement. Tara liked to handle tricky situations with low-key intensity. Maggie liked to blow them apart.

"Secrecy," Maggie whispered gleefully as she sat down across from Tara at a tiny table in a back corner. "I love this intrigue. You always choose the most unknown eateries in Manhattan."

"I *try* to keep our meetings safe," Tara told her wryly. "For your benefit."

"Phooey!" Maggie set a sleek eelskin purse on the scarred linoleum table and leaned forward, her eyes gleaming with curiosity. "How are your interviews going with Ethan?"

"Fine, as far as the *Constitution*'s business editor is concerned. We've met four times during the past two weeks. I ask questions for the business section, and Ethan answers them graciously. And every time I come up with some brilliant and sly maneuver to wheedle information about Logan's campaign to make smoking sound harmless, he sidesteps it. The man deserves a doctorate in diplomacy."

"Ah, yes. You should see how he controls the board of directors. Never a false step! And even when you think you've cornered him on a question, he slips away from you. I can never tell which side he's on. Sometimes I could swear that he supports my eccentric views on diversification. But the rest of the time I'd bet my Neiman-Marcus card that he's as old-line as the rest of the board. The man's quite frustrating."

A waitress appeared to take Maggie's lunch order. Tara sipped a cup of coffee and ruefully agreed with her assessment of Ethan. Frustrating, definitely. Since the scene in the stables at Dunverary, he'd been on his best behavior. They met for the interviews in undisturbing, public places—museums, libraries, even Central Park—and his manner was always the same. Unerringly polite, always intense, but never overtly personal.

He relaxed her, and she knew that he *meant* to relax her, but not too much. The provocative way he looked at her when he was discussing mundane subjects undermined the safe, businesslike atmosphere. He leaned toward her when he talked, and when she talked, he listened with head tilted and eyes riveted on hers. He was, in effect, mesmerizing her.

"I'm going to do one more interview with him," Tara told Maggie. "I let him talk me into dinner this time."

"And then?"

"And then...that's all. No more meetings."

"But you've made inroads, Tara! You've broken his reserve a little! If you keep going—"

"I'll be in significant trouble. Personal trouble." The truth was that she had already crossed the boundaries of personal trouble, but she didn't want to admit it.

Maggie's open-mouthed assessment turned into a long *ohhh* of understanding. "You and Ethan..." She let her voice trail off. "What a perfect combination."

"Oh, good lord, Maggie. You're hallucinating."

Maggie squinted at her shrewdly. "Yes, yes," she affirmed, nodding. "I see it now. He's the kind of man who would naturally be driven to distraction by your cool, standoffish intellect. And you're the kind of woman who has tremendous admiration for people with strong convictions. Even if they're contrary to your own."

"Which hardly means that we're the perfect romantic couple—"

"Hmm. A grand thing. Yes. What a relationship!"

Tara sighed in defeat. Maggie had settled the issue, as far as Maggie was concerned. "I'll invite you to the wedding," Tara muttered ruefully.

Maggie smiled. "I can't wait."

"Don't hold your breath," Tara warned.

At five-thirty, Tara took her briefcase and headed for the elevator. Downstairs, she hurried across a lobby decorated with glass-enclosed displays of the *Constitution*'s most famous front pages. She had just one hour to go home and change clothes before she met Ethan. Her simple beige suit wouldn't do for the elegant restaurant he'd suggested. An unrepentant part of her also acknowledged that she wanted to look beautiful tonight. Their last night.

She pushed through the revolving doors to the street and paused, blinking in the spring sunshine as she looked for the nearest available cab. At first, she didn't notice the black stretch limousine parked on the curb in front of her.

But her gaze flickered to it in amazement when one of the doors opened smoothly and Ethan stepped out. He came toward her, a devilish smile curving one corner of his mouth, his tall body perfectly displayed in his trademark black suit with gray pinstripes. He held out a hand for her briefcase.

"Your coach awaits, Cinderella."

"Good heavens!"

"Come along."

He took her briefcase and the raincoat she held over one arm, helped her into the limousine, then settled beside her. A uniformed driver appeared and shut the door, closing them inside a secluded world of tinted windows and plush leather. Ethan handed her a glass of champagne from the ledge of a gleaming bar that faced their seat. He took a second glass for himself, clinked it to hers and said jauntily, "I altered our dinner plans a little."

Still in shock, Tara took a large swallow from her glass. "I need to go home and change into my glass slippers." He smiled. The limousine pulled noiselessly into traffic.

"I thought as much. I gave the driver your home address. We'll stop by."

"Do you know *everything* about me?"

"Hardly." He looked at her from under his brows, the indication being that he intended to learn many more personal details besides her address.

"And what else have you *altered* about dinner, fairy godfather?"

"Fairy godfather? I'm the *prince* in this scenario."

"That remains to be seen."

He chuckled. "Ungrateful wench. I'm taking you to the best country inn in upstate New York. You're about to have the most tempting dinner of your life."

She suspected that he wasn't referring simply to food. "Ah, I see. The perfect spot for a business interview."

He waved one hand in dismissal. "We'll take care of that on the trip up. Now, drink your champagne and get in the mood to be wined and dined."

And seduced? she wondered silently, and took another large swallow from her glass.

While Tara changed clothes elsewhere in her condominium, Ethan moved slowly around the small, immaculate living room, studying every detail. The furnishings were modest but comfortable—framed watercolors on the walls, a simple couch upholstered in slate blue, a well-worn smoke-gray recliner beside a reading lamp, an oak coffee table spread with everything from *Scientific American* to *Better Homes and Gardens*. It was a homey place full of personal mementos, and he liked it.

With methodical inspection he noted the contents of the crowded bookcases that covered the walls. Here were clues to her vulnerable, personal side, and he intended to glean as much as he could from them. He decided that she enjoyed the VCR atop her small, console television, because the bookcases contained dozens of homemade tapes. He scanned their labels, smiling to himself.

So she liked the Three Stooges. Ethan continued his perusal of the shelves. *Dr. Zhivago* and *Thin Thighs in Thirty Days* competed for space among several sets of encyclopedias, numerous biology and medical books, and a variety of paperback novels. A shelf full of framed photographs suddenly grabbed his attention. Ethan touched each photograph with a fingertip, as if he could absorb Tara's life that way.

Her sisters were pretty, homebody types, smiling among their husbands and children. Her mother posed patiently in front of a small frame house with well-tended shrubbery, a friendly dog lolling at her feet. Her father looked stalwart and handsome in his dress Air Force uniform.

Ethan sighed. He envied Tara this traditional, all-American family. But she was a loner, just like him. She'd had to leave everything behind and attack the world by herself. She was the restless one in her family, the same as he was in his. He felt a deepening sense of unity with her.

Abruptly, Ethan found himself looking at a photograph of Tara with a tall, lanky man. She had an arm around the man's waist, and he was laughing. She smiled tentatively, like a person who didn't feel comfortable at the center of a camera's attention. The presence of the Statue of Liberty, mist-shrouded in the background, confirmed that the picture had been made in New York. Ethan had little doubt that the man was McGee Webster.

Come home, you damned hypnotist, he ordered grimly. So Tara can get on with her life. Our life.

Ethan replayed in his mind what he intended to say to her on the way home from dinner tonight. It was risky, but he had to trust her. If his plan worked, there'd be one less obstacle between them. If it didn't . . . well, what was the appropriate phrase? Fool for love, Ethan noted. Love.

"And what information have you deciphered about me?" she asked drolly as she walked into the room.

Ethan turned slowly, his eyes eager for the sight of her. Pleasure and pride made him warm as he noticed the deliberately tempting way she'd dressed for this evening with him. His eyes swept down a flowing white dress that draped gracefully over her curves. An ornate red belt and red high heels added rich color to it. She carried a tiny red purse and a white shawl. Her jewelry consisted of a simple gold necklace and matching earrings.

"You're beautiful," he said. "But I already knew that." He was pleased when she couldn't hide an appreciative smile.

"Flatterer."

"Never. I speak the honest truth."

"Flatterer," she said again, and reached for her briefcase.

"Please, let me tote and fetch for you, Cinderella." Ethan smoothly snatched it from under her hand. "Pardon me while I domineer once again." His expression teasing, he gestured toward the door. "To the coach."

Chuckling, she walked past him to the door and waited while he opened it with a flourish. "I'll be interested to see if it turns back into a pumpkin."

"Ah, Cindy, have faith in my princely powers."

Oh, Ethan, I wish I could, Tara thought wistfully.

Downstairs at the limousine, he handed her briefcase to the driver. Tara turned her back for a second, fiddling with her shawl as the driver opened the door for them. Suddenly she felt Ethan's large hands on her shoulders. "Allow me," he said languidly. "You needn't lift a finger for yourself tonight. I'll handle everything."

His touch brought instant awareness to nerve endings throughout her body. Tara glanced over her shoulder, feeling his presence as if he were holding her close. "I'm sure you mean that in a professional sense," she quipped. He merely smiled.

"Have you ever seen *Holiday Inn*, with Bing Crosby?" she asked as they sipped espresso after dinner.

"I've never been to a movie with Bing Crosby."

Tara laughed softly and shook her head in rebuke. The combination of champagne in the limousine, wine with dinner and Ethan's warm, teasing attention made her feel as if she were floating on a cloud, carefree. "You know what I mean, ridiculous person."

"No, I've never seen *Holiday Inn*," he offered in fake contrition.

"Well, the point is that I thought inns like this only existed in movies." She glanced around at the candle-lit dining room with its country-French ambiance. Aromatic wood crackled peacefully in a stone fireplace. Thick rugs made colorful islands on a wooden floor. In one corner, a harpist played the most ethereal music Tara had ever heard. What a lovely fantasy, Tara thought in bliss.

"I agree," Ethan murmured.

She looked at him in surprise. "Did I say that out loud?" Smiling, he nodded. "Oh, dear. Too much wine."

"No. Just enough." He put his espresso cup down and extended a hand. "Let's dance."

"To harp music?"

"Be adventurous."

Her cup rattled a bit as she placed it on a saucer. "Neither of us has a halo."

"That's what makes us such a perfect pair."

Unable to argue with that provocative comment, Tara took his hand and he led her to a small clearing in front of the fireplace. She moved, suddenly breathless, into his arms. He slid his arm around her waist with just the right amount of possessiveness—enough to excite but not startle. He curled her hand against his shoulder and drew her close. As their bodies met, Tara gazed up at him with half-shut eyes and parted lips.

"You could ruin me with a look like that," he whispered. They barely moved, their dance floor confined to a square foot of space, their world a cocoon of emotion and desire.

"I don't want to ruin you," she whispered back.

"Too late. I'm already ruined. You're responsible, and I'd like to know what you're going to do about it."

Tara was vaguely aware of her body merging tighter with his and good sense dissolving in the magic of the moment. "Perhaps I'm a little ruined, too," she said in a soft, pensive voice.

He knew her confession was precious, a fragile admission that she regretted having to make. "Sssh," he murmured, soothing. If all went well later, he'd make her regrets fade. For now he was content simply to touch his forehead to hers and hear her sweet sigh in response. After a tentative moment, she rested her head on his shoulder.

"Dancing is uncomplicated," he said against her ear. "Let's just concentrate on that."

Tara nodded into the warm, dark hollow of his neck. A part of her knew that reason and reserve would return soon. A part of her fought that knowledge. Ethan was one contradiction after another, a confusing mixture that made her want desperately to ignore principles and professionalism. She would, for now. Just for now she let her senses absorb everything about him and she gave life to the bittersweet thought that hid just inside the harp: I wish I could let myself love this man.

"You've been quiet for the past hour. Quiet is not necessarily good," he said with forced lightness as the limousine slipped along a dark country road.

"I'm a quiet person. And I like listening to your stories about the constellations." In the shadows, Tara relaxed deeper into the soft leather seat. The interior of the limousine was faintly illuminated by the stars and moon of a beautiful, clear night. And she didn't want to say what had to be said, she thought with an ache of sorrow. Goodbye.

"I don't bore many people with my fascination for astronomy," he quipped. "In fact, it's not what I usually discuss with a beautiful woman."

"I'll take that as a compliment."

"It is."

Tara laughed softly. "I'm not bored."

"But you're not content, either. I can hear those principled little wheels clicking in your mind." He straightened his tie with an absentminded gesture, as if preparing for a speech. "It's time for dessert," he said gruffly.

Tara stiffened warily, wondering what he intended. "Ethan..."

"Just listen," he told her.

She twisted to gaze at him in bewilderment, her hands clasped in her lap. "What is this all about?" she asked anxiously.

"It's about trust. It's about truth." He settled back in his corner of the seat, ran a hand through his burnished hair and cleared his throat. "It's about time you understood how things really are with my position at Logan Tobacco."

Long minutes passed as Tara listened in stunned silence. He had been forced to assume leadership at Logan. He was loyal to Killihan Logan and the company Killihan had so lovingly built, and that was the primary reason he had submitted to the board of directors' subtle coercion. At first he had hoped that once he stabilized the tobacco company he could gracefully step aside, perhaps to take over CEO duties at one of the conglomerate's other divisions. But he'd become indispensable in the board's eyes, and now he was trapped. They made it clear that he had only two options: remain at Logan Tobacco or leave the conglomerate entirely.

"So I decided to beat the board at its own game," he told her. "I'm going to move Logan away from the tobacco business—but slowly, very slowly, to give the industry's economic dependents time to adjust. Of course, I have to play the middle line, in order to keep the board on my side. I have to convince them that they *want* to diversify our holdings. One day, when we have so many other lucrative ventures that tobacco provides weak profits in comparison, I'll win."

"You mentioned the industry's *dependents*," she said slowly. "Such as your brother, the tobacco farmer?"

Ethan nodded. "Such as Noah and thousands of people like him. Even if I had the power to shut down Logan's factories tomorrow, I wouldn't do it." He paused, his eyes seeking hers in the low light. "But I *will* do it eventually, Tara. You have to believe that."

As if coming out of a dream, Tara struggled to absorb the impact of this confession. He was giving her the most precious gift he had. He was giving her his confidence and his trust. She could ruin him with this information, and he knew it. If it was true. She gazed at him in a haze of confusion. Was he setting her up, deliberately feeding her false information? But why would he tell her things that could only hurt him, and Logan Tobacco, if that were the case? He was saying that he wasn't immoral, that she'd been wrong about his principles. She wanted to believe him with every shred of hope in her soul.

"Ethan," she began hoarsely.

"Ssssh. Let me finish. I'm not an idealist—"

"Ethan, I don't understand why you're doing this—"

"Cinderella, I have to get this off my chest. I'm not an idealist, like you are. I'm not a moralist. But tobacco has become an indisputable villain, a controversial, slowly dying industry in this country, and I won't let it drag the Logan name down." He sighed. "Now, here are some details that will support what I've just said."

"You've told me enough," Tara blurted. "Please don't say any more."

Ethan stopped in midsentence. "It's important that you know."

"I'm a reporter, for God's sake. You shouldn't tell a reporter things like this. Ethan, some reporters don't keep their off-the-record interviews confidential. There's no law that says they have to. It's just professional courtesy."

"*You* wouldn't abuse a source that way."

"How can you be absolutely certain? What you've told me is very valuable information."

"I *have* to trust you, Tara. I *need* to trust you. I don't have anyone like you in my life...anyone worth taking that risk for."

"You must have business colleagues."

"That's not the same, and you know it. You know what I mean. I want to fill my life with you. I've always felt...incomplete...and now I know why. I've been waiting for you."

Spurred by emotions she didn't take time to analyze, Tara leaned forward and grasped his hands. She asked desperately, as if she didn't want to say the words, "What if I don't believe what you've told me?"

He wound his fingers tightly through hers. Suddenly he dipped his head and touched his mouth to her parted lips. His breath was warm and tempting as he spoke against them. "Is it so difficult for you to believe that I'm not a villain?"

She was trembling now. "I've never said you were a villain."

"Believe what I told you. I wouldn't make up lies in order to seduce you." He paused. "I want the truth to seduce you. Can I trust you with it?"

She didn't mean to let the soft sound of encouragement escape from her throat, but it did, a bittersweet whimper that summed up her decision. "*Yes*. Always."

Her yearning tone drove Ethan to take her in his arms and taste her mouth again, seeking her blessing in ways she couldn't resist. Self-denial had left her ripe for this—not for just any man, but for him, for passion and commitment that would shake them both to the soul. He saw her loyalty to McGee Webster as misguided but heroic, and it made him want her even more. He wasn't taking her from a man she still loved; of that he felt certain.

Her hands shook as they crept around his neck. He felt their quivering as she touched the skin above his collar, and the knowledge that he affected her so strongly almost destroyed his control. He wanted to crush her to him, and he fought to keep his embrace gentle. He stroked her back through the soft white dress, noting the strong, athletic curve of it, the slope of it into the slender waist girded by her belt.

Oh, yes, she was strong—in both the physical and the emotional sense—but there were vulnerable spots in her armor, and he would find them. He would give her his own vulnerability in return.

Ethan groaned hoarsely as her mouth opened like a sweet mystery. She surrounded his tongue with welcoming softness, damp and arousing, the essence of feminine invitation. The urgent forces in him responded with unleashed acceptance, probing her secrets with deep, quick strokes.

She speared her fingers into his thick hair and pulled his head closer, then suddenly cupped his face between her hands. Her fingertips feathered over his cheeks, as light as spring rain and incredibly sensitive. She mapped the slight coarseness of his skin with a delight that made him feel exquisitely wanted.

Their bodies pressed together, the angles and curves in harmony, and only the awkwardness of their side-by-side positions kept them from merging in an even tighter embrace. They traded small, impatient sounds that came from deep in their throats. Tara felt the rough vibration from his mouth to hers, and it thrilled her. For the first time in her life, she understood the reckless, purely emotional forces that commanded fulfillment despite all odds.

"I said once," he whispered, skimming his lips over her cheeks and nose, "that I would steal you."

And Tara knew that she was nearly at the point of letting herself be stolen. Her voice hoarse, she begged him, "Stop!" and tilted her head away from the wild temptation he offered. Her caressing fingers pressed into his jaw, holding him away as she tried to regain sense and reason and principle. "There's still so much to consider—"

"And so much to anticipate."

"Please."

But instead of letting her go, his body quivering, Ethan guided her head to his shoulder and buried his face in her smooth, dark hair. She put her arms around his neck and clung to him, breathing raggedly. "We can't go on like this," she murmured. "We *shouldn't*."

"We have to," he replied, kissing her hair, nuzzling it, inhaling her light perfume and a sweet scent that was uniquely feminine and uniquely hers. "Slowly, if you want. But Tara..." He rested his cheek against her hair and shut his eyes. "We can't walk away from something this special. It would be sacrilege."

He felt her shudder, and her fingernails dug into his shoulders. "I thought it would be so simple to say goodbye when the interviews were finished," she murmured sadly.

"Nothing is simple between us, Cinderella. Nothing ever will be."

"I know that now." Gently but firmly, she pushed herself at arm's length from him. His hands trailed to her rib cage, his thumbs daringly close to the soft undersides of her breasts. In one easy, upward movement, he could have cupped them. The darkness was now broken by the quick strobe of passing streetlights. The limousine had entered Manhattan and would soon arrive at her high rise. His eyes burned into hers, and her breath shattered the silence with a soft exhalation as he leaned forward and took her mouth again.

Tara's back arched compulsively as the pressure of his fingers commanded her to participate in one last moment of abandonment. This time the kiss was so light and lingering that Tara found it even more erotic than before. He teased her with what he withheld and all that he promised. When he drew back, he let his hands drop to her waist. Tara weakly brushed her fingertips across his wide, serious mouth, and he nibbled them. He dipped his chin and studied her thoughtfully.

"I'll be out of town for the next few days," he said. "And that will give you time to think about all we've discussed tonight. About Logan. About ourselves. I'll be back by Friday."

Think. Yes, Tara considered with a rush of bittersweet anxiety. She needed time to think. If what he'd told her was true, he had given her power over his company, his career and his life.

Six

———

The square digital clock on her office desk had just flashed 10:00 a.m., but Tara was already on her fourth cup of coffee for the day. Missy and Larry sat across from her desk, scribbling notes to themselves about their upcoming stories. Tara looked down at her master list of topics, her eyes gritty. She hadn't slept much in the three nights since her dinner with Ethan.

"Ah, here's a good lead," she told them. "A new study links heavy caffeine intake to behavioral problems in pre-teens." She glanced up to find the staff writers coyly arching their brows at the mug in her hand. Her mouth flattened in a rueful line. "I passed puberty a few years ago. You don't have a *thing* to worry about."

"We never said a word," Larry protested, his face filled with merriment.

Missy shook her head and smiled pleasantly. "It never entered our minds that you might be the miscreant who scrawled that message on the door to the men's room in the sports department."

"What message?" Tara asked.

Larry grinned. "The one that said, 'Quiet. Sports Staff Conference Area.'"

Missy laughed heartily. Tara couldn't help smiling. She put her mug down and pushed it behind a stack of medical journals. "Just to protect my reputation, I'll switch from caffeine to sugar." She opened her desk drawer and retrieved a candy bar.

"Boss!" Missy exclaimed. "You said you were giving up sugar! What happened to homemade yogurt and fresh fruit and—"

"They've got no preservatives," Tara interjected. "I realized that I need my preservatives."

She had just unwrapped the candy bar when Harvey Bergen marched through the open door. "I came for my last Ethan Boone tape," he announced.

Tara put the candy down slowly, feeling her hand quiver for reasons that had nothing to do with too much coffee. She gave Harvey a solemn look. "No, of course you're not interrupting, Harvey. Come right in."

He rolled his eyes. "I wouldn't impose if you'd brought the tape to me promptly. Where is it? Is it damaged? Did you lose it?"

"Is this a game show, Harvey? Do I win a blender if I give the correct answer?"

"Dear, obnoxious woman, is my simple request too much for you to comprehend?"

"Watch out," Larry growled. "Or we'll tie you to the rest-room door down in sports."

"Now, *that* would be more disgusting than graffiti," Missy added.

Tara stood up, shushing her protective staff writers with a slight gesture of one hand. Harvey's face, as was typical, had turned red. She opened her desk drawer and removed the tape of her business interview with Ethan. "Here you go, Harvey. Last one. I've put one in the computer. If you want a transcript, just let me know. I asked him every question you gave me about Logan's mentor program for junior executives. An interesting subject."

"Could you pry any personal information out of him? He was Killihan Logan's fair-haired boy, I understand. Personally, I suspect that Boone waited until the old geezer became senile and then used him as a stepping stone."

"You have a cynical mind, Harvey." Tara bristled with a protective urge so intense that it surprised her. She wanted to tell Harvey the details of Ethan's relationship with Killihan Logan, but she couldn't. To admit that she knew all sorts of personal information about Ethan would be to open a Pandora's box of questions.

"Harvey's not cynical. He's a pervert," Larry said pleasantly. "A minor difference."

Harvey shot him a killing glare, stuck the cassette tape in the pocket of his Brooks Brothers shirt and stomped out.

"Oooh, I love it when Harvey stomps," Missy commented. "He's nearly masculine."

Tara sat down, frowning. From a professional standpoint, her decision to protect Ethan was completely correct, because he'd spoken off the record. The fact that she adored the man only added strength to an ethical commitment. There was nothing wrong with that, was there? Tara rubbed her temples and felt shards of pain shoot through her scalp. "Let's finish up here," she told Larry and Missy. "I'm getting a headache."

"It's caffeine," Larry noted.

"It's sugar," Missy suggested.

It's the knowledge that I'm putting my professional credibility on the line for Ethan, Tara corrected silently.

* * *

That afternoon as she scanned a completed column on her computer screen, a phone call came from Julia Gibson in the newspaper's legal department.

"You've been saying your prayers at night," Julia told her cheerfully. "Logan has dropped the restraining order on those memos from its medical experts. You can print them."

For a second Tara sat in stunned silence. "Did they say why they dropped the order?"

"Well, we had a good chance of getting it overturned, and I'm sure they knew that. But... who knows? The Logan attorney who called me gave the usual song and dance—how the company has nothing to hide, et cetera ad nauseam—but I suspect that it was an arbitrary decision on someone's part there. I'm amazed."

Tara thanked her for the news and hung up. Ethan was responsible for this new development, she felt certain. She picked up her phone pensively. It was Friday, which meant that he was back in town. Tara punched a number that connected her with Ethan's assistant, Dora Brown.

"Mrs. Brown, this is Tara Ross. I hope you're doing well today. May I speak to Mr. Boone, please?"

Good phone etiquette never swayed Dora Brown. "Mr. Boone will be in meetings for the rest of the afternoon. I'll be happy to take your message."

Tara shut her eyes and exhaled slowly. "All right. Please tell him this. 'As you requested, have scheduled another... interview. Please meet me this evening, seven p.m., The Crazy Italian.'" Tara quickly gave the restaurant's address. "And tell Mr. Boone... that Cinderella appreciates the return of her glass slipper."

"Cinderella...appreciates the return...of her—I beg your pardon?"

"Glass slipper," Tara repeated, her cheeks coloring. "He'll understand."

* * *

Casual. She had to look casual. As she shifted from one-foot to the other by the door of The Crazy Italian, Tara's nerves radiated tension. Maybe Ethan couldn't make it. He hadn't called in response to her message. But then, he'd been in meetings. Maybe he'd been busy all afternoon. Maybe he'd be here in a minute. It was exactly seven o'clock. Maybe I'll chew my nails, Tara thought wryly.

She checked their muted red polish for chips. She straightened her blue pullover and fiddled with the collar of the white blouse underneath. She smoothed her crisply pressed jeans and studied her white flats for scuff marks. Stop it, she told herself. She focused her concentration on the glowing marquee of the theater across the street. Breathe deeply and relax.

A silver-gray Jaguar slid into a parking space a few feet past her. All hopes of breathing deeply or relaxing fled as she watched Ethan unfold his tall body from the Jaguar's front seat. His gaze was riveted to her as he locked the door and walked to the sidewalk. There was so much to say that she couldn't say anything but simply locked her gaze to him as he came toward her.

He wore designer blue jeans that were undoubtedly not as old as they looked. His torso was a masterpiece of male geography in a beautiful V-necked sweater, white with a bold red-and-black pattern across the chest. His heavy gold wristwatch, the kind that included a bewildering array of gadgetry, caught the last glints of sunlight. Sleek brown loafers encased his feet. He mixed casual and classic on a mature male body in its prime. The combination of his overwhelming physical appeal and the magnetic emotion in his eyes was hypnotizing. He stopped only inches from her, searching her face with a look so open and intense that it drew goose bumps to her skin.

The anxiety flowed out of her, leaving a quiet, almost contented feeling. "I believe I owe you a debt of gratitude," Tara murmured. Silent understanding stretched between them like a gossamer web.

His rugged face, so capable of looking stern, relaxed into a pleased smile. "I wanted to give you a lift."

"I know." She couldn't resist a jaunty response. "I would have gotten to print those memos from Logan's medical experts eventually, anyway."

"Yes, you would. Otherwise, I'd never have let you have them without a fight. I wouldn't jeopardize Logan."

She looked at him askance. "What about the things you told me the other night?"

"That was between us. That was personal, and I trust you with them, as I said then."

Unadulterated pleasure made her smile as she absorbed the respect and faith in his blue eyes. "You really *do* like to take risks, don't you?" she said, shaking her head.

"You won't hurt me, because you care about me. You're not the kind of person who can hurt someone who means a great deal to her." He laid on broad warm palm against the side of her face and, with his thumb, rubbed lazy circles on her cheek. "You asked me out on a date tonight. I like that."

"This is not a date," she protested smugly, waving one hand at the restaurant. "It's just a truce dinner."

"The first of many."

"Now, Mr. Boone, don't get carried away—"

"Let's just enjoy each other's company tonight. Let's just talk and be friends. There's so much I want to learn about you." He slipped his arm around her waist and pulled her to his side with playful roughness.

Emotion nearly made her dizzy. "Friends," she repeated as they walked into the restaurant. It was an interesting new possibility, and a deceptively harmless one.

They opened up to each other slowly, over dinner. Eventually he told her more about his youth; scrapes with the law, periods in juvenile detention centers, dislike for a father who was either moody or absent. When he revealed, finally, that his father had died after being shot by a jealous girlfriend, Tara understood why it had been so hard for him to discuss his past that day at Dunverary.

She confessed to being a little driven and competitive. He laughed then and said he'd suspected *that* for some time. Tara explained that her parents had demanded good grades and encouraged perfectionism in all three of their daughters. After her father's death in Vietnam, her mother required even tougher personal standards, as if to honor him.

"I was the only girl in my high-school class who carried a bottle of antacid in her purse," Tara told Ethan. He listened with his hands steepled against his mouth, his eyes relaxing her with their empathy. Tara's memories of those years weren't particularly happy, even though she loved her parents. "I admit, however—now that I'm grown—that I'm better off for having been raised that way."

He lazed against the back of their red vinyl booth and studied her with shrewd eyes. "Would you put your own children through such misery?"

Tara gave him a rebuking look. Then she sighed with defeat. "No. Never."

"Good."

"And how do you want *your* children to grow up, Dr. Spock?"

"Happy. Confident. Responsible. Sensitive to the feelings of others. I'll settle for that."

Tara tilted her head to one side and looked at him quizzically. A sweet feeling of pride warmed her inside. "That's a very mellow philosophy. You harbor no urges to create a corporate dynasty?"

He shrugged. "I'm proud of what I've accomplished, but I wouldn't force it on my children. I want them to have choices that I didn't have."

"Such as?"

He cleared his throat—looking, she thought, a little embarrassed. "Astronomy. I would have made a helluva Carl Sagan type."

Tara inhaled softly. "You still could."

"Maybe someday."

"Would it be so hard to leave the Logan conglomerate?"

He looked at her steadily. "Yes. I've spent most of my life involved in it. I've given it so much of myself."

Tara pretended to watch her thumb trace paths in the cool sweat of her beer mug. "And what do you have left?"

He didn't answer right away, and she looked up to find invitation and challenge in his eyes. Her mouth curved in a gently teasing smile. "Warning: cliché ahead. Is it lonely at the top?"

"That's for me to know and you to find out." His voice dropped as he said, "Takes one to know one."

She smiled to cover her uneasiness, determined not to let intimacy complicate friendship. "Nice clichés you've got there."

"Is your career all it promised to be?"

"So far. I'm happy."

"Happy with your life?"

Tara stole the last slice of pizza from the pan between them. "Hmm. Pizza. I can't do without it. How's that for irony? A health and science writer who craves cigarettes and loves junk food."

He watched her take a bite and chew vigorously, as if she was really paying attention to taste. "You're human. It's acceptable to be less than perfect."

Ethan stroked the side of his jaw with one finger, a sensual gesture that made her newly aware that his features were too strong to be classically handsome. That didn't make them less appealing, though. Less than perfect, but perfect, she decided.

"It's acceptable to want and need something simply because it could give you a great deal of pleasure," he added. "Something—or someone."

"I want and need another glass of beer."

He smiled ruefully. "You're fantastic at diplomatic maneuvers."

"I'll take that as a compliment from the master. I've heard how you can run board meetings."

Chuckling, he refilled her mug from a pitcher they shared. "Maggie Logan tells you a lot about me, does she?"

Tara nearly choked on her pizza. She squinted at Ethan and tried to determine an appropriate response.

He shook his head. "I told you the day we met that I suspected Maggie was your source of inside information. Don't squint at me behind those dark eyelashes and try to appear inscrutable. It's all right. I won't do anything about it, because—overzealous though she may be—Maggie and I are on the same side. She just doesn't know it. And I can't tell her. What I'm doing is too delicate." He paused. "And I hope you won't tell her."

It was pointless for her to deny that Maggie was her source. Tara nodded. "You and I have been trading quite a few secrets lately," she mused, shaking her head. "Neither of our employers would approve."

"I like trading secrets with you. This is just the beginning," Ethan assured her.

"Of a nice friendship."

"That's only one part of it."

He waited when she shook her head again, her eyes troubled, then she said, "It's not as simple as that. You have to understand something." Tara was silent for a moment, considering how to best arrange her guilt into words. "I still . . . I encouraged McGee Webster to take an assignment in Lebanon. I don't know if he would have gone otherwise."

"Then you *were* breaking up with him," Ethan stated softly.

She nodded wearily, knowing it was pointless to pretend otherwise any longer. "I was. But...we were still very close. When he left, he said he hoped we still had a chance. And I told him I hoped so, too."

She closed her eyes for a moment, then opened them to find Ethan's searing gaze analyzing every emotion that crossed her face. "But we didn't. I knew it then, but I couldn't say it."

Ethan rested his hand on hers in a soothing way. "Your compassion for him is something I admire and respect. I hope he's alive and that he comes home. But there's no need for you to put your life on hold because of him."

A knot tightened her throat, and she looked at Ethan wistfully. "I haven't made a conscious effort to be...celibate. It's just worked out that way."

"Because you've been too honorable to let yourself look twice at a man until you know what's happened to McGee."

Tara gave him a bittersweet smile. "I looked twice at *you*, and it's gotten me into a great deal of trouble."

He nodded and then chuckled softly. He knew they both wanted to lighten the mood, and he took the opportunity. "And will get you in a great deal more before the night's over."

Tara arched one brow at him. While she struggled to make some sensible rejoinder to that remark, Ethan tossed money on the table and stood up. "This was my treat..." she began.

"Oh, no. I want you to be obligated to me." He looked at the ceiling as if in deep thought. "What do pizza and beer warrant? A smile? A little hand-holding?"

"Sounds so innocent," she replied dryly.

He held out his hand and nodded toward the exit. "Let's go have dessert at the frozen yogurt shop down the street. It's a wonderful spring night. We can walk."

She answered as if speaking to herself, "All right. So I'm easily obligated by pizza and beer." Then she took his hand, stood up and gave him a broad, exaggerated smile.

He laughed. "It's a start."

It was nearly midnight when they sauntered back from the yogurt parlor. The May temperature was perfect, and the air held an invigorating mixture of city scents: of food from the neighborhood restaurants, of crowds as people poured out of a theater nearby, of the cars and trucks that jostled along the wide street. The scents of happiness and excitement, of *life*, Tara thought giddily. Or perhaps, she conceded, she was simply infusing the night with the magic of her mood. Ethan swung her hand playfully, his fingers entwined with hers.

"And then," she told him, grinning, "Moe poked Larry in the eyes—you know, with that great sound effect, *poink!*—and Curly went 'Nyuck, nyuck, nyuck,' and Moe turned to *him* and thumped him in the forehead—*boink!*—and I just fell off the couch laughing! It was their best scene ever!"

Ethan chuckled richly, his eyes gleaming at her with affection. "Why do I suspect that you adore Saturday-morning cartoons, too?"

"I do! Especially the old Bugs Bunny and Roadrunner series."

"Now, *I* prefer something more sophisticated." He paused, nodding proudly. "Reruns of *The Beverly Hillbillies* and *Green Acres*."

"No!" She laughed. "That's unbelievable!"

"I'm a Southerner. What can I say? Those shows are in my blood."

"Don't ever offer to be a blood donor!"

"Why, you . . ." He grabbed her by the waist and began to tickle her. Chortling happily, she tried to squirm away, but suddenly he bent and scooped her into his arms. Kicking her feet and grabbing frantically on to his neck, Tara gasped with laughter as he whirled her around. He set her down but kept her close to his side with an arm across her shoulders.

"Trying to frighten me?" she demanded as they started walking again.

"Trying to confuse you," he answered devilishly. "Trying to make you forget good sense."

Tara felt as if she'd already done that. She flung one hand up and chucked him lightly on the chin. "It won't work!"

"Resisting will get you nowhere." He dipped his head toward hers, and his smile became sensuous and tempting. "Kiss me."

She raised her face, her wry smile wavering, her gaze on his slightly parted lips. "Kiss you, eh?" He brought them both to a halt. She touched her mouth to his.

"Look out!" a man yelled desperately.

Ethan jerked his head up at the sound. Tara's gaze followed his to a small yellow car that bounced over the curb and careered down the sidewalk in their direction. Fellow pedestrians flung themselves out of the way as the car's driver tried desperately to steer. His eyes trained on the car, Ethan grabbed her by both shoulders and shoved her toward the street. Tara's heart turned to ice as the onrushing vehicle rebounded off a building and came straight at them.

She grabbed Ethan's sweater and threw herself to one side, trying to tug him while he tried to push her. She was dimly aware of his adrenaline-charged arms around her. He twisted violently, scooped her up and vaulted toward a car parked by the curb. The yellow car was nearly on top of them now. Tara's senses burned with acid fear. There was no time, no time.

She felt the gathering of incredible power in Ethan's body and realized abruptly that he was going to jump onto the hood of the parked car. When he did, she felt as if the world were exploding under them. He landed on the car's hood at the same instant that the yellow car bumped it. Thrown off balance, still holding her tightly, he fell on his back, and Tara heard the air leave his lungs. She clung to his neck as he tumbled off the car's far side.

Then, suddenly, the melee was over. Tara realized that, wonder of wonders, Ethan stood at the edge of traffic, which had come to a hurried halt. He had landed on his feet and still held her clasped to his chest as if the whole routine had been part of a carefully planned acrobatic act. Horns honked. People got out of their cars to whistle and applaud his nonchalant heroics. But Tara heard his ragged attempts to draw breath and felt his body trembling wildly. Gasping also, she drew her head away from his shoulder—how it had gotten there, she couldn't remember—and looked at him weakly.

He was already gazing down at her, his anxious eyes squinted almost shut with the exertion of trying to regain his breath. Behind them, the driver of the runaway car, a young man, was exclaiming that his steering had failed, that he was an actor, that actors didn't know anything about steering mechanisms.

"Down, d-down," she finally ordered, since Ethan seemed unaware that he could let her go now. His arms loosened and she slid, wobbly-kneed, to a standing position beside him. Holding on to each other, they sat on the fender of the parked car that had saved them. He gulped for air, his broad chest moving spasmodically.

"C-Cinderella," he managed, and took several more breaths, "that kiss had one *helluva* kick."

Overwhelmed with the conflicting need to laugh, cry and kiss him, Tara did all three. Ethan had rescued her. He was holding her as if he'd never let her go. He wanted her in his life regardless of problems and risks. And she wanted him, too. Silently, gently, tears running down her face, she said goodbye to the memory of McGee.

Tara and Ethan sat in the Jaguar and watched the police

direct curious people away from the car that had gone out of control. The actor sat morosely on the steps of a nearby building, reading his handful of traffic tickets. A police officer walked to the Jaguar and bent down to gaze at them through the open window on Tara's side. "You guys can leave, if you want to. Sure you don't want us to take you over to the emergency room for a checkup?" This was the fourth time he'd tried to talk them into it.

Ethan shook his head. "We're fine, officer. But thank you."

"How about you, ma'am? Are you sure?"

"I'm fine, too, officer. Not a scratch."

"Okay." He frowned. "You can take off, then."

As the cop got into his patrol car, Tara turned to Ethan solemnly. They shook hands. "We were very convincing," she told him. "I doubt he suspected that we share an aversion to X-ray machines."

"And doctors with cold hands," Ethan added. Smiling tightly, he shut his eyes and let his head settle back on the driver's seat.

Tara studied his profile and watched his squint lines deepen into a grimace. Alarmed, she placed a hand on his arm. "Ethan? What's wrong?"

He swallowed slowly, and his smile faded. "I'm *not* going to the hospital. I ... just have a sore back." Now that the officer was gone, he shifted his legs a little and winced. Tara saw the tentative, stiff way he moved and knew that he was in considerably more discomfort than he was admitting.

"Ethan! You've been pretending!"

"Ssssh." He laughed softly. "Did I tell you about the time a few years ago when I tried to climb a pine tree out in Colorado?"

"No, but what—"

"I was wearing snow skis. And traveling at about twice the speed of sound."

"Oh, Ethan, are you telling me that you've aggravated an old back injury?"

"Would I angle for sympathy that way?"

"Can you drive?"

"Certainly." He straightened in the seat and studied the Jaguar's floor shift and clutch. "Any minute now." Then he laid his head back on the seat and shut his eyes.

Tara inhaled sharply in sympathy. Then she patted his arm and got out of the car. She went around to the driver's side, opened the door and held out both hands. "Come on, Gramps. Let's trade places."

Moving very slowly, he swung his long legs out of the car and grasped her hands. "I love strong women," he quipped in a voice that strained for lightness. She helped him out and walked with him, one hand on his back, as he eased his way around to the passenger side. When they were settled in their new places, he fished a set of keys out of a front pocket on his jeans.

Tara took them nervously, trying to remember when she'd driven last. It was the last time she'd been to Nebraska for a visit, months earlier. She'd borrowed her mother's car to go shopping. And that, unfortunately, was the only time she'd driven in recent years. She hadn't owned a car since her arrival in New York, when she'd discovered that monthly parking fees were roughly the equivalent of a house payment in Omaha.

She squeezed Ethan's hand. "Where, precisely, do you live, Gramps?"

"Upstate, about forty-five minutes away."

Tara groaned in defeat and cranked the car. "How would you like to spend the night at my condo? It's only about five minutes from here?"

He turned his head so that he could look at her. He chuckled hoarsely. "If that's an indecent proposition, the answer is yes."

Tara clucked reproachfully. "I'll give you some tequila and a back rub. I respectfully submit that you are wildly overconfident to consider anything else, Gramps."

"A back rub?" he said with a hopeful smile.

She nodded. "I worked my way through college as a masseuse in a women's health spa. I was licensed, even."

"A licensed back rub! And tequila!" He faced forward and sighed. "You're my kind of doctor. Are your hands warm?"

All of her was warm right now, Tara thought ruefully as the Jaguar jerked into traffic under her inept guidance.

Seven

The sight of Ethan stretched out on his stomach on her living room floor made Tara come to an abrupt halt just beyond the kitchen door. "*Why* did you get off the couch? And *how* did you take your sweater off without help?"

"Very carefully," he quipped, his chin resting on his arms. "The couch wasn't long enough. My feet hung over the end."

"It was made to accommodate patients of medium height."

"Come here, doctor, and do your duty." He groaned softly, turned his head to one side and closed his eyes.

Tara hurried over and knelt beside him. In the soft light from the floor lamp beside her recliner, his back was a map of intriguing shadows. She scanned the broad, tanned expanse of it. Muscle flowed into muscle with mesmerizing symmetry. A patch of dark blond hair accented the curve of his lower back and disappeared under the waistband of his jeans. He was a big man, and there was nothing boyish about the powerful, trim lines of his body. He had kicked off his loafers and lay with his legs spread slightly, his bare feet nestled in the thick cream carpet. Tara allowed herself one glance at the way his long thighs tied into angular hips.

"Staring at the patient with an unprofessional eye, are we?" he mumbled. She looked quickly at his face and saw a sly smile replace some of the pain around his mouth. Tara checked the coffee table by the couch and confirmed that he'd drained a double shot of tequila from the tumbler that sat there.

"Tipsy, are we?" she replied.

"Pain medicine. Don't badger the patient."

She had gone in the kitchen to wrap ice in a towel. Now she gently laid the cold compress in the curve of his back.

"Ahh. Cold back, warm heart."

Chuckling, Tara went into her guest room and pulled a pillow off the bed. She ruefully surveyed the room's clutter. In the small condominium, it was the only storage area she had. The bed was piled with boxes and stacks of magazines.

"Lucky man," she told Ethan as she helped him arrange the pillow under his head. "You get to sleep in *my* bed tonight. The servants forgot to neaten the guest bungalow."

"I bribed them to forget." He paused. "Hmm. And you're going to sleep with me? You should. I'm harmless."

She smiled ruefully but tingled at the thought of sharing a bed with him. "Ethan, if you were in traction with both legs and arms broken, *maybe* you'd be harmless. I'll sleep on the couch."

"Why?" he asked seriously, his voice a low rumble.

He was simply referring, without teasing, to the inevitable. A part of Tara accepted the fact that they were going to become lovers, that she *wanted* to make love to him, but it was still such a new admission that she wasn't ready to discuss it. "I'm an animal," she said drolly. "I might take advantage of your innocence."

"I *have* no innocence."

"Then *get* some."

She pinched his shoulder lightly, and he made ouching sounds. To make up for hurting him, she spread her hands on the pinched spot and began to rub. He sighed happily. Tara felt her stomach drop as the warm surface of his skin slid under her fingers. She straddled his hips and pressed both hands against the top of his spine, stroking outward. After a few minutes, Ethan began to laugh low in his throat.

"Oh, I *love* this," he said with languid delight.

"I'm so glad," she retorted dryly. But she couldn't help smiling.

Silence enveloped them again as the slow, caressing massage progressed. Tara stared fixedly at her fingers, watching them glide over bone and sinew, feeling his muscles bunch and relax with sensual response. She worked her way up to his neck and pressed her thumbs into the edge of his blond hair. The beautiful harmony of light and dark shades entranced her, and she let her thumbs slip into its silkiness. Her mind wandered as she imagined how the other side of him, with that powerful chest and flat stomach, must look.

"You're squeezing me with your knees," he said softly.

Tara blushed as she realized that she was indeed clenching her legs to the sides of his hips. Her thigh muscles burned a little with the strain of keeping herself from sitting on his backside. She scooted down and worked on the middle of his back, drawing her fingertips along the center of his spine.

"Tara?" he said in a gruff voice. His Southern accent was heavier now, and her name sounded as if it had been dipped in honeyed liquor. No man had ever said her name with more erotic effect.

"Yes?"

"That day at the Vietnam memorial. That was a good moment."

"I remember," she murmured gently.

"We weren't strangers."

Her hands forgot that they were giving a therapeutic massage. She squeezed his sides in affection, telling him that she'd sensed a bond between them, too. "I thought you were the kindest person I'd ever met," she said.

"And I thought you were the bravest."

Resistance was beginning to desert her. Tara bent over him and placed a kiss between his shoulder blades. He trembled and tensed. "Here now," she said in a husky voice. "We're getting off track." She leaned away and worked her hands farther down his back.

"Did you believe everything I told you the other night, about myself and Logan Tobacco?"

"Yes." She sighed, wishing she could think of some logical reason why she had accepted his confession so easily. Tara admitted silently that she had wanted to believe in him, to trust him, since the day they met, and now she relied on instinct alone to tell her that she could. It was enough. Thinking about the way he'd saved them both from the car earlier, she glowed with pride. His life was built on a foundation of ideals that his cynical nature preferred not to admit. She knew that, even if he didn't.

Tara laid the ice compress aside and pressed gently into his lower spine. "Nice lordosis you've got here. In, um, layman's terms, the lordosis is the curve of your back."

"Would you like to see more of it?" Without waiting for her answer, he raised his hips a little, reached under himself and unsnapped his jeans. Then he put his hands back by his head, on the pillow.

"A small amount will be sufficient for massage purposes." Her heart pounding, her senses fired with the realization that she wanted to touch and kiss all of his magnificent body, Tara hooked her thumbs under the waistband of his jeans. She found the edge of his briefs and caught them, too. Then she tugged the materials down an inch or two, exposing more of the attractive patch of hair and the top of his hips. "Ah, a tan line," she said, trying to tease, her voice rough with arousal. "So you don't wear low-cut swimsuits."

"I'm not a show-off," he protested coyly.

"Oh, yes you are." She ran her hands over his silky flesh and watched the hair part around her fingers. Her palms conformed to the valley of his back and then rose with the curve of his rump. Her breath caught in her throat. "A man's skin is so different from a woman's. Rougher. Ruddier."

He whispered, "When I touch your hands and face, I always notice how delicate you feel."

She laughed softly, pleased. "I'm not delicate." Tara heard her desire expressed in the husky tones. "But thank you." She continued to massage his lower back.

"You're delicate in ways a man would notice." He shifted a little. Tara abruptly realized that he was as aroused as she, and the floor provided no accommodation. Bone and muscle seemed to dissolve inside her, leaving a delicious, heavy feeling.

"What ways would that be?" she breathed.

"Would you like to have a family one day?"

She wasn't certain how that tied into what she'd asked, but it was a pleasant subject. "Mm-hmm. Children. Pets. A house with lots of trees and a big lawn." She laughed lightly. "A membership in the PTA."

"Delicate. That's what I mean."

Tara laughed again, and he joined in with his baritone chuckle. She lightly clasped her hands to the top of his hips, extending her fingers just under the edge of his jeans. Seeming to know what she wanted, he gingerly lifted his hips an inch. Her heart bumping in a thready rhythm, she slid his jeans and briefs down to his thighs. His movements painful, he drew one knee up a little to ease his contact with the floor.

The air seemed to sparkle with intensity. Tara tentatively rested her hands on his bared rump and felt the rounded pads of muscle quiver. But a charmed little smile on his lips told her he was comfortable with the vulnerable, undemanding role, and that knowledge made tenderness well up inside her. His power and strength lay not in dominance, as she had once thought, but in confidence. He understood that a man could be passive without being weak.

"You're very impressive," she told him, meaning it in so many ways. Tara curved her hands to fit him and slowly slid them to his spine again. She watched her splayed fingers move up and down the matching halves of his back, dividing his pain in two and coaxing it away. They talked more, of simple things, friends and daydreams. It seemed perfectly natural for him to lie there with most of his body exposed. Then they stopped talking, and she felt him quiver from time to time.

He was in pain, Tara thought anxiously, and she made her touch more of a caress. Her worry grew as she saw that his contented expression was fading. Finally she asked, "Does your back feel any better?"

He lay with his head turned so that she could see only the left side of his face. His eyes were shut tightly. He nodded.

"But I can tell that you're very uncomfortable. Oh, Ethan. Ethan."

"Shhh. It'll be fine by tomorrow."

Tara watched wretchedly as unhappiness was carved into his features. "What can I do? Would you like to soak in a hot bath while I rub some more—"

"No!"

With his large hands he knotted the pillowcase. "Ethan?" She put her fingers on either side of his ribs and noted the rapid rhythm of his breathing and heart rate. "What's wrong?"

"Stop, please." He sounded frustrated and sad. He was silent for a moment, fighting some inner battle. "This isn't . . . a game, anymore."

"I never meant it to be—"

"Don't you understand?" He hesitated, his jaw working. "I want to make love to you so badly that I could cry."

Her emotions crested in a symphony of devotion. With a hoarse, soothing sound, she stretched out beside him. He put his left arm around her and drew her head close to his, on the pillow. She kicked off her flats and draped one leg over his. He sighed and tried to smile. Tara kissed his eyelids, his nose, the lines of fatigue around his mouth, and then that grim, tired mouth itself. Decisions are suddenly so simple, Tara thought with deep, sweet confidence. She hadn't expected this, but it was right.

"Let me make love to *you*," she whispered. He opened his eyes slowly, so close to hers that she could see tiny flecks of silver in the blue. They were mature eyes, with lines at the corners and underneath. For the first time, she saw how desperately the soul behind them could hurt and hope. Tears came to her eyes. "Turn over," she instructed him tenderly. "Just be still and let me touch you."

"But it won't be any good for you that way."

She shook her head, smiling at him in affectionate rebuke. "Making you happy would be *very* good for me."

His eyes gleamed with adoration. They never wavered from her face as she rose on one elbow. She held his head to help him move more carefully and kept her gaze tight on his, offering encouragement. When he was stretched out on his back, he drew her down to him for a slow, intimate kiss that was equal parts gentleness and urgency. He put one hand beside her face and she twisted her lips into his palm, kissing the warm hollow of it, her eyes shut, her face turned toward his nakedness. He trailed his fingers off her cheek, and she sensed that he was waiting for her appraisal.

Tara opened her eyes slowly, taking the sight of him in small degrees, every second flooded with excitement. His chest was covered in a luxurious cushion of hair, the same rich blond color as that on his back. His skin had the kind of weathered look that came from athletic hours in the sun, not from a tanning booth. Her gaze followed her fingertips as they moved down to the flat earth-brown discs of his nipples. She circled each with her nail, and Ethan's rough inhalation signaled the immediate effect.

"Delicate," he murmured. "Your touch . . . incredible."

His stomach was a taut plain terraced with small muscles. "Charming," she whispered as her fingernail circled his navel. He tried to laugh, but the sound caught in his throat. Tara looked farther down his body, and her hand trembled. She whispered her admiration, and Ethan's breath shattered the silence of the room in a sigh of delight. He groaned, and she heard discomfort as well as pleasure. Tara realized abruptly that the small of his back was unsupported.

"Shhh," she soothed him. Tara twisted around, half knelt and retrieved a throw pillow from the seat of the recliner. "Arch your back a bit." When he did, they were both aware of the hearty bounce the movement produced in another part of his body. Tara's face burned with pleasant embarrassment, the kind that was easy to share. "Come hither, the master says," she quipped.

He laughed softly as she slid the pillow under him. When she began to tug his jeans farther down his thighs, he raised his head and gazed at her with weak protest. "Ye lustful wench, will ye remain clothed yet have me totally naked?"

She nodded blankly as she studied the hairy, muscular thighs that her work was revealing. "I wish but to make ye totally *comfortable*, sire."

"Oh, Tara," he said hoarsely, all playfulness gone. His head fell back on the pillow and a long shudder passed through him. "I've lived my whole life waiting for you."

She was amazed at the suddenness with which tears slid from her eyes. She finished removing his clothes, then lay down beside him quickly and burrowed her face into the crook of his neck.

"Tara?" He wrapped both arms around her and held as tightly as his sore back would allow. "Honey, what's the matter?"

Honey. The endearment made her tears flow faster. At the same time, she began to smile and shake her head in self-rebuke. She drew back a little so that she could look down at him. He frowned as he searched her wet face for answers. "I'm *happy*," she assured him, wiping her eyes with her fingertips. She gestured vaguely, trying to sum up her feelings. "It's just that...this is one of those exquisite times...when you know *exactly* who you are and what you want and that life couldn't be any better."

"What do you want?" he asked in a voice drenched with tenderness.

"You," she barely whispered, and kissed him. She cupped one hand under his head, threading her fingers deeply in his soft, thick hair. She trailed the other down his body and boldly wrapped him in pleasure, stroking with a slow rhythm.

His body shifted convulsively from her skilled, uninhibited attention. He tore his mouth away from hers and gazed up at her with his eyes half-shut and his face flushed with desire. "Nothing like this has ever happened to me before," he rasped. "Lying here, naked, in the arms of a fully clothed woman who's—Tara...it'll happen so fast if you don't stop—"

"There'll be many other times, later," she promised in a tone so loving that he groaned in happy response. He grasped at her back, winding his hands into her sweater, releasing them frantically, then sinking them into her hair. He jerked her mouth down on his and kissed her roughly, his tongue taking her as he wanted to with his body.

Tara responded wildly, losing all sense of self, knowing only that her body was melting inside her clothes, that he was making love to her as surely as if they were joined, that a shattering demand was building at the center of her womb. The feel of him, hard and pulsing inside her hand, gave her more pleasure than she'd ever imagined possible. He gripped her rump fiercely, and Tara curled against him, moaning into his mouth as the world disappeared in a rush of beauty.

Shivers cascaded through her, making her head bow beside his, her hair draping over his face, her breathing harsh. Ethan's scent was her scent, the light sweat that dampened his shoulder and her cheek was her sweat, Ethan's life was her life. When he moaned her name and let his body arch recklessly, she shared the euphoria that overshadowed his pain.

Neither of them could speak; Tara tried, and watched him try, but finally they shook their heads in unison and simply held each other. She tenderly curled her fingertips into the sweaty hair on his chest as if she could absorb him through her skin. He wound his fingers through hers. She angled a leg between his, and he nuzzled his face into her hair. They fell asleep, him naked, her clothed, both of them new.

The May dawn drifted into Tara's bedroom window through white mesh curtains. The faint golden light was just beginning to warm Ethan's face as he opened his eyes. He blinked slowly, enjoying the delicious half sleep that lets pleasant dreams mingle with reality. Only, this morning reality was more precious than any dream. He lay very still, letting it come to him in small, wonderful ways. The fragrant scent of Tara's hair; its softness against his jaw. The satiny feel of her breasts brushing his arm as she breathed slowly and deeply. She lay on her back; he lay on his side, his top leg thrown across her thighs.

He smiled crookedly. This was the way they'd fallen asleep. Had neither of them moved? Of course, he recalled, they had come into the bedroom a few hours ago. They'd awakened on the living-room floor, both of them cold and stiff. He'd practically tumbled over her, leaning on her as she helped him into the dark bedroom. After he'd lain down, she'd rubbed his back for a long time. And then she'd sat quietly, lifting one hand occasionally to stroke his hair as he undressed her. She'd lain down beside him then, her body as naked as his, and he had whispered compliments into her ear as he'd explored her in the dark with his hand.

Now he raised his head and looked down at her, smiling. Her mouth was relaxed in an inviting way and her hair was tousled sexily. He couldn't imagine her looking cool and businesslike anymore. She could retreat behind that facade at work and for other people, but never again for him. He knew her too well. Cinderella, he teased her silently.

Ethan frowned as he acknowledged another reality. He wanted her, and his body had, in fact, awakened him specifically to make love to her. He closed his eyes and tested his sore back by arching it a little. He sighed with relief to find that it was adequately agreeable. As he shifted, the evidence of his need pressed against Tara's soft thigh. Ethan cursed silently. He was going to wake her up with romance, not lust, he chided himself.

He quickly looked at her face, hoping she was still sound asleep. But her dark lashes fluttered, and her lips pursed lazily. Ethan held his breath, enchanted but also afraid that he'd notice regret or surprise when she opened her eyes. Slowly her lashes unveiled the soulful green eyes he cherished. As if sensing his concentration, she focused directly on his face. Her mouth curved into a blissful smile. Ethan felt that his chest might burst with delight.

She shifted her leg languidly, and Ethan reached between himself and her to cover his reaction. "Don't. I like it," she whispered, the words barely audible. Her eyes were gleaming now, soft and full of desire.

His Tara, he thought, feeling blessed. When the time was perfect, he was going to say the words that had been on his mind for so long: *I love you.* But he didn't want to say them in bed—not the first time he spoke them. He didn't want her to worry that they were just lust words, spoken to make sex more polite. For now he repeated them silently as he gazed down at her.

"Ethan," she murmured, his name an invitation. "Ethan."

Shivering from emotion, he took her in his arms and kissed her with infinite care, treating her lips as if they were fragile. This morning he took charge, and she made it clear that she wanted him to. As he let his lips trace every contour of her face and neck, she stretched and curved under him, making tiny, whimpering sounds in her throat.

He made it the best for her. He made the prelude last forever, until she was moaning under his mouth and hands, her head thrown back and her eyes hazy with passion. A stream of sunlight dappled the carpet by her queen-sized bedstead, then edged up the legs, then reached his and Tara's naked glistening bodies. As the light turned them both to gold, Ethan sheathed himself in her magic. It wasn't possible that he could love anyone or anything more than her. It wasn't possible for her not to love him in return. She clung to him in the sun, chanting his name. Afterward she lay quivering in his arms. "More," she whispered. And there was more. "Forever," she whispered. And they made each other feel immortal.

Tara moved contentedly around her small, pleasant kitchen, a yellow silk robe wrapped around her body. She filled the dishwasher, put soap in its dispenser, then shut the door. She turned toward a counter, searching distractedly for something, then clasped her forehead with one hand and began to laugh. "I put the philodendron in the dishwasher!" She opened the door again and removed a lush plant in a white ceramic pot. "Sorry, Philly. I meant to water you, not wash you. I was daydreaming."

And she had so much to daydream about. Ethan had been with her since Friday night, and it was now Sunday afternoon. Her body was deliciously tender from all their lovemaking. Her kitchen was a mess from the Italian dinner they'd concocted last night. As a chef Ethan was magnificent but sloppy. Of course, when one combined fondling and kissing with cooking, she thought wryly, sloppiness was acceptable. She laughed again, feeling giddy.

Tara tiptoed through the condominium and peeked into her bedroom. Poor darling, he'd earned a nap, she thought tenderly. She'd worn him out. He was sprawled on his stomach, the blanket and sheet twisted low around his waist, one long, gorgeous leg uncovered. He had his head burrowed in a pillow, and his hair was sexily rumpled. Sections of *The New York Times* and the *Constitution* were scattered around him.

They'd spent the morning in bed, reading the papers and discussing various articles. Eventually their attention had returned to more personal interests. Afterward he had sighed happily and told her that the Arts and Entertainment section had been aptly named.

Feeling domestic and loving it, Tara hummed as she straightened up her living room. A videotape of *Wuthering Heights* lay on the coffee table. Two empty wineglasses were upturned on a magazine. Pillows and blankets were jumbled on the couch. She smiled at the evidence of a wonderful evening. As Tara carried the glasses to the kitchen, she heard the telephone ring in the guest room, where she kept a phone and office desk for after-hours work.

Trying to let Ethan sleep, she ran to her bedroom and softly shut the door. Then she hurried back to her makeshift office, frowning. Who would call her business number on a Sunday? She didn't want to think about work today. "Hello?"

"Tara! Tara, dammit! This is Harvey!"

Her frown turned quizzical at the fury vibrating in his voice. "Thank you for calling," she replied lightly. "But I'm not interested in purchasing a subscription to *Irate Men Monthly*." She heard the sound of something being thrown against a wall and the sound of a chair squeaking as a body shifted in it.

"I'm sitting here looking at a computer terminal, Tara! I'm looking at *your* file!"

Stunned, Tara was silent for a moment. No one *ever* sought access to another editor's files without permission. It was newspaper policy. "What are you doing in my directory? That's confidential and you know it! That's against every rule—"

He laughed tersely. "Can the histrionics, sweetheart. You have a lot more to worry about than my infraction of the rules! My deadline got moved up and I had to work today. I needed your transcript of the damned Ethan Boone tape. And guess what other interesting file I found when I was perusing your directory."

Suddenly Tara's knees refused to support her. She knew exactly what he meant, and she sank into the chair beside her desk. Nausea made her put one hand over her stomach. "And which file would that be?" she asked in a low, desperately neutral voice.

His answer came back slow and victorious. "The one that says that the CEO of the largest tobacco company in the world wants to stop selling cigarettes."

Eight

Tara moved leadenly into the bedroom. She stopped by the bed, tortured with guilt, and watched Ethan sleep. The agony inside her made breathing difficult. Thinking was horror. She made herself face it, and a shudder went through her. He'd never forgive her, she thought in anguish. She'd never forgive herself.

Tears burning her eyes, she studied him with a tormented expression and put one hand over her mouth to stifle a choking sound. He was so peaceful, so beautiful. The moments she had shared with him over the past weekend were the best she would ever know, and soon they would be all she had left. She hurt as if a sledgehammer were raining blows on her back. She had to have one more minute with him.

She forced her tears away and took a ragged breath, then knelt on the bed and crawled to his side. She lay down next to him and stroked his gleaming hair with a hand that tried desperately not to shake. "I love you," she told him, mouthing the words. She knew it now. Tara felt as if her neck would snap with the tension as she nestled her face close to his and pressed a kiss to his mouth.

"Hmm." He smiled, his eyes still shut. She put her arm around his bare shoulders and held him tightly. "Hmm."

Moving lazily, he pushed the covers down and drew her closer, burrowing his head against her throat, his lips seeking her warm skin. He nibbled delicately and slid on top of her. Tara parted her legs and felt the satiny material of her robe slide up as his large body settled in the harbor of her thighs. He was sleepily affectionate but not aroused. He cupped one of her breasts and rubbed the nipple with his thumb.

Let me just hold him, she prayed. Let me just hold him like this, gently, so that he'll remember, later. He has to remember. She wound her arms and legs around him and hid her distraught expression in his golden hair. He angled his head upward so that he could tickle her earlobe with his tongue.

"You snuck out of bed when I wasn't looking," he protested in a husky whisper.

She couldn't force her throat to form an answer, so she hugged him tighter. His other hand was under her, caressing her shoulders through the robe.

"Have you ever been to Europe?" he murmured.

"No," she managed after a moment, her throat on fire.

"I dreamed about you and me, in Europe." His breath feathered her ear as he chuckled softly. "Italy. Do you think the Leaning Tower of Pisa is a phallic symbol?" He sighed and hugged her tenderly. "I think we should go to Italy someday. And France. I've been to Paris on business, but God...to be with you, in Paris...in the much-fabled springtime..."

Tara couldn't bear any more. The beautiful scene he painted would probably never come to life now, and the knowledge tore her apart. Tears slipped from the corners of her fiercely shut eyes. Racked with shudders, she dug her fingernails into his back and turned her head away from his.

His response was immediate and anxious. "Honey, what is it?" He rose on his elbows and grasped her face between his hands. "Tara?"

"Let—me—Can't breathe—" He moved off her quickly, and she tugged her head away from his ministering touch. Before he could reach for her again, Tara slid to the far side of the bed and sat up, her shoulders hunched and her face buried in her hands. Tell him now! she ordered herself. Simple, direct words! She groaned, hoping that, like a sharp knife, the words would at least cut cleanly.

"Tara?" he said desperately.

"My business editor knows what you told me about diversifying Logan," she said in a low, dead voice. "I put some notes in a computer file at work. He found them."

Awful silence filled the room. The mattress shook as Ethan jerked upright.

"What?"

"I made...notes...about our conversation in the... limousine. About...everything. The way you feel about tobacco products, the way the board of directors forced you to accept the CEO position at Logan, how you...hope to move the company out of the tobacco business eventually."

She heard his harsh inhalation, then he said, "You kept a *record*? When you *knew* it was just between the two of us?"

Tara pressed her fingertips into her temples and nodded wearily. "It was just for myself."

The air seemed to crackle with his growing shock and anger. "But you didn't *need* a record. Why would you need to keep notes on something that no one but you and me was ever supposed to know?"

"I'm a writer. A writer keeps notes on *everything*."

His voice vibrated with emotion. "If she plans to use them someday she does."

Tara whipped around, shaking her head miserably. "No!"

He was leaning toward her, his fists clenched in the sheets, his eyes narrowed in a squint of pain and disbelief. "You left those notes where someone could find them."

"Oh, Ethan, not intentionally! I swear!" She pounded the mattress with a fist. "My computer directory is supposed to be restricted. Everyone's at the newspaper is!" She gulped for breath. "We each have secret passwords, and I don't know how Harvey Bergen got access to mine. He'll have to answer for it—"

"And after a meaningless reprimand he'll publish an article based on your damned notes!"

She groaned. "No, no, not if I can do anything to prevent it. What you told me was off the record. I'll explain that to my managing editor, to the executive editor—to the publisher, if need be."

He slapped at the air, dismissing her words with a vicious gesture. His voice was sarcastic. "Do you think that will do a damned bit of good?"

"I don't know." Defeated, she let her shoulders droop. She gazed at Ethan without hope or spirit. "But I'll try my best." She laughed bitterly. "If it makes you feel any better, I'm in danger of losing my job for withholding the information from Harvey."

Ethan rammed a hand through his hair and looked at her with anguish and fury. "Dear God, how could you be so careless?" he whispered hoarsely. "Do you know what a story like that will do to Logan on the stock market? Not to mention what it will do to my relationship with the board. I'll be damned lucky if I can accomplish anything, after this. *If* they don't force me to resign."

She no longer cared whether she defended herself or not. Tara felt as if she had nothing left inside, nothing to keep her from crumpling. Her body swayed a little, and she said nothing. He vaulted off the bed and went to a chair where she'd neatly folded his clothes. She knew his back was still tender, but she saw that any discomfort was forgotten now.

Without looking at her, he jerked his jeans on and zipped them. His shoulders shook as he took deep breaths. He snatched up his sweater with one hand and jammed his feet into his loafers. Then he swung around to confront her again, his arms rigid by his sides. Tears ran down his face. Tara put her hands up in despair.

"Whether this screwup was deliberate or not, the fact is that you mishandled the confidences I gave you. You didn't care enough to protect me," he rasped, his words barely audible. He swallowed with difficulty. "You didn't care."

"Oh, no. No! Ethan, don't walk out of here believing that!"

"You didn't need to make notes about what I told you. Your *foolish* professional pride—" he fought for control "—has ruined both of us."

"I'll make everything right, if I can."

"You can't. You'll never be able to correct what you've done." He slung a hand across his cheeks and the old mask of reserve settled over his features. They were no longer lovers, no longer friends. They were only two people who shared a bottomless well of pain.

"Let me go with you! Whatever you're going to do, let me stay with you!"

"I'll have enough to contend with, without having to worry what you're going to do next." His movements brusque, he put his sweater on. "And you're the last person I need to be seen with."

Tara hugged herself and bent her head. She had expected his bitterness, had girded herself for it, but struggled now to accept it. "Whatever you want me to do, I'll do it," she whispered raggedly.

"I want you to stay away from me."

She gave him a stricken look but got only a cool stare in return. Tara closed her eyes for a second and nodded. He walked to the door and paused, looking at her, his jaw working harshly. "Stay away from me," he repeated. "I don't want to see you...or think about—" Breaking off with those tormented words, he turned and left.

The *Constitution*'s executive conference room was a cool, tastefully businesslike place of sleek furnishings and deceptively warm track lighting. Impersonal—perfect for this group, Tara thought grimly as she faced the newspaper's hierarchy. At the far end of the table sat Arrica Pennington, the publisher. Tara wished that Mrs. Pennington were like the lovable matriarch from *Lou Grant*. Unfortunately, Mrs. Pennington was more like Joan Crawford in *Mommie Dearest*.

"I can only conclude, Ms. Ross," Mrs. Pennington said in her husky, Boston-bred voice, "that you developed an unprofessional relationship with Mr. Boone."

Tara didn't falter. She would keep her pride in this fiasco, at least. Her chin up and her eyes calmly on the publisher's, she nodded. "It was personal, but it wasn't unprofessional."

Dan sat near Tara, fiddling with a pen. He cleared his throat. "Exceptional circumstances," he grunted. "Tara is one of the best. I vouch for her, Mrs. Pennington."

Tara shot him a grateful look. Some managing editors would have backpedaled furiously to escape blame for a situation like hers. The seriousness of the problem was evidenced by this meeting of top management. Beside Dan, Harvey arched one brow and smiled smugly.

"You, Mr. Bergen, have nothing to smile about," Mrs. Pennington interjected coldly. "Your decision to invade another editor's computer directory cannot go without penalty. As of today, you are no longer eligible for salary increases or promotion. The period of suspension is up to Dan's judgment."

Harvey blanched. Tara tried to feel a sense of victory, but she felt so drained that she merely gazed at him without expression. Penalizing Harvey would do nothing to help Ethan.

"As for you, Ms. Ross," Mrs. Pennington continued. "You are hereby demoted to staff writer. Effective immediately."

Tara nodded apathetically. "My only interest is in protecting my source. His information was given off the record, and I'm asking you not to publish it." Dan had already told her that her request was hopeless, but she had to make it.

"Did Mr. Boone ever specifically state that his remarks were not for publication?"

"No, but it was unmistakably implied."

"I don't think implications are binding, Ms. Ross—"

"My *sense of ethics* is binding, Mrs. Pennington."

"And I'm sure that you're aware of the importance of the Logan Tobacco story. Mr. Bergen, would you elaborate for everyone here, please?"

Harvey had a cruel look about him that told Tara he was going to enjoy hurting her. "Think what would happen if the chairman of IBM wanted to get out of the computer business. Or if the CEO of Coca-Cola said he despised soft drinks and planned to stop selling them. The stock market ramifications alone are important. The story has national— even international—scope."

Disgust burned under Tara's rib cage. She gave Harvey a look of distaste, then turned a cutting gaze at Mrs. Pennington. "That's all true. But let's face the real issue," she said softly. "We can't let ethics stand in the way of selling newspapers."

Mrs. Pennington's eyes glittered with anger. "I have no urge to argue ethics with a disgruntled employee."

Tara stood up. "Arguing ethics with you would be like trying to teach a pig to play the banjo. I'd waste my time and annoy the pig." There were audible gasps among the executives around the table. Tara turned gracefully toward Dan. There was only one thing she could do to repay Ethan for all the harm she'd done him. It had been in the back of her mind since he'd walked out, two days ago. "You'll have my letter of resignation within thirty minutes."

"You'll be missed," he said immediately.

Without a backward glance, Tara left the room. Goodbye, career, she thought numbly.

Tara stayed at the office until the end of the day, helping a tearful Missy and an irate Larry prepare to carry on alone. They wanted to take her out for drinks, but she gently refused. Drinking would only intensify her misery. Carrying a bulky cardboard box full of her belongings, she went downstairs for the last time and pushed through the lobby doors. It was a gorgeous spring afternoon, so fresh and promising that it made her ache. And sitting at the curb was a long black limousine. Tara gasped and took a step backward as Sam, Ethan's driver, came toward her across the sidewalk.

"Mr. Boone would like to speak to you for a moment, please," he said politely. He held out his hands for the box.

Tara gazed at the limo's mysterious dark windows, her heart racing at the thought that Ethan waited behind them, that he was undoubtedly watching her reaction. Trembling inside, she let Sam take the box. He opened the door to the limousine, and she was so nervous that she stumbled as she got in, crunching her ankle against the curb.

Tara didn't feel the pain. Her attention was riveted on Ethan, who sat in the far corner of the limousine, his legs crossed and his expression aloof. He wore a charcoal-gray suit and a dark tie with a gold collar bar. The French cuffs that shone at his wrists were fastened with magnificent onyx links. He radiated icy power.

She smoothed a hand over her navy herringbone suit and was glad she'd worn a dressy white blouse with it. Her outfit was stylish and appealing, and today she needed all the ego-boosting she could get. She had trouble breathing past the knot in her throat.

"So you were fired," Ethan said flatly.

He appeared neither pleased nor sorry. Tara realized that he'd drawn his conclusion from the cardboard box, and she hesitated to answer, thinking, Why tell him that she resigned in noble anger? It wouldn't change anything between them. And she didn't want him to feel sorry for her.

She shrugged. "I thought you didn't care to see me."

"I want to know when to expect the article to appear. You owe me that information. No one told my PR people that."

"Tomorrow. I'm sure Harvey tried to reach you today for a rebuttal."

"He did. The public relations people are handling it."

Tara clasped her hands in her lap and sat rigidly on the edge of the seat. "I assume that you're already fighting for your corporate life."

"Yes."

Silence stretched between them as blue eyes burned into green ones. She wanted so desperately to touch him that her hands hurt with the effort of remaining still. "Is that all?" she asked in a strained voice that failed to conceal her sorrow.

His eyes, guarded and half-shut, flickered over her as if he were reassessing everything he saw. They stopped on her ankle, and Tara glanced down. Her hose were torn, and a trickle of blood colored a large, scraped place. She drew her gaze up quickly as he reached over his shoulder and tapped an intercom button on the limousine's door. "I'm getting out here, Sam," he told the driver. "I want you to take Ms. Ross home." He gave her address brusquely, then opened his door.

"You don't have to—" she began. His raised hand and cold glare stopped her.

"Don't confuse the offer with anything personal." With that hurtful remark, he twisted his body and got out of the car. Sam arrived at his side and closed the door for him, shutting Tara inside the quiet space alone. She leaned her head on the leather seat and watched with dull eyes as Ethan stepped into a cab. He never looked back.

In the darkness, Tara focused on the glowing tip of her cigarette and exhaled a long stream of smoke. Wearing only her robe, she lay on the couch, a telephone receiver propped against one ear. Tears slid down her face as she listened to Maggie Logan.

"If anyone could talk himself back into the board's good graces, it would be Ethan," Maggie assured her gruffly. "Logan stock will stop fluctuating as soon as the timid investors have been calmed by the public relations people. Today they had Ethan personally issue a statement that categorically denies everything the *Constitution* printed, including the part about diversification."

"How is he, Maggie?" Tara cleared her throat roughly. "They're making him say all sorts of things that he hates, aren't they."

Maggie's voice was troubled. "Yes. He's scheduled to be interviewed by Ted Koppel on *Nightline* this evening. He'll be interviewed on CNN tomorrow." She paused. "So. Has the newspaper come to its senses and begged you to return?"

Tara took another drag off the cigarette and pinched the bridge of her nose as fatigue and nicotine sent a wave of dizziness over her. Maggie, too, thought she'd been fired, and Tara wasn't going to correct the impression. She didn't feel like listening to anyone tell her how self-sacrificing she'd been to resign. "It's time to move on," she murmured. "Next week I'll start putting out feelers."

"What are you doing this week?"

"Smoking. Sleeping. Smoking. Eating. Smoking."

"Tara, the irony of this is mind-boggling. You and Ethan . . . tobacco . . ."

"I feel sick, Maggie. I'll call you tomorrow."

"Sick?" Maggie sounded alarmed.

"Just nauseated. I'll be all right. Have to go—right now—bye."

"Bye."

Tara ran to the bathroom and threw up. Then she got her carton of cigarettes, methodically opened each pack and spent the next fifteen minutes flushing them. She smiled darkly. Didn't like them anyway, she thought. I only smoke Laramies. And since that was a Logan brand, she couldn't bring herself to buy any. She sat on the bathroom floor, hugged her knees to her chest, leaned weakly against the cool white bathtub and fell asleep.

When she woke, she glanced at her wristwatch and discovered that *Nightline* was already in progress. Tara hurried to the living room and switched on her television. When Ethan's face appeared on the screen, she sat down on the floor and touched his image with her fingertips.

He was answering a question about medical statistics and smoking. To the world, he was relaxed, confident, devastating, the kind of man who made the best-dressed and most-eligible-bachelor lists and the Fortune 500 achievement lists. To her, he was tormented, and it showed in his eyes.

"The *Constitution* report is based on erroneous second-hand information," he told Ted Koppel. "I have no personal antipathy toward smoking. Logan's medical experts have conclusive evidence that the dangers of smoking have been exaggerated and that no clear link exists between smoking and disease."

Tara groaned and shut her eyes. He might regain his credibility with Logan's board of directors and stockholders, but at an enormous loss of personal integrity. Even when his position was secure again, would he have a chance of accomplishing all the idealistic goals he'd secretly set for himself? Because he was brilliant and indispensable, the board could be coaxed into forgiving, but never into forgetting. They'd always be wary.

Ted Koppel was talking now. "Your public relations people claim that the remarks you made to a *Constitution* editor were taken out of context and misinterpreted. The newspaper told us that the editor in question has been placed on leave of absence. Your people say that this is clear proof that unprofessional conduct was an issue. Do you agree with that?"

Tara held her breath as Ethan's eyes narrowed. "No," he said flatly. "As far as I'm concerned, it was just a matter of misunderstanding. There were no intentional improprieties."

"Oh, Ethan!" Tara buried her face in her hands. A commercial intervened, and she switched the television off, unable to bear any more torture. He'd defended her, she thought with poignant tenderness. Despite everything, he'd defended her. She loved him dearly, and he didn't even know it. She stumbled to her bedroom in the dark and lay down atop the quilted blue coverlet, curled up on her side like a distraught child. Sleep, when it finally came, contained bad dreams.

The next morning she was forcing down a breakfast of sugary pink cereal—usually her favorite junk food—when the building's security guard buzzed the intercom by her door. Tara went to it wearily, her head echoing the buzz.

"Yes, Bill?"

"A George Bennett is here to see you. From the State Department. Can he come up?"

Tara stared at the intercom with sick dread. Over the past two years, George Bennett had been her contact person for news about McGee. Even though there had been no news, she and George had stayed in touch. But he had never visited her before. "Yes," she said in a small, frightened voice.

As soon as she opened the door and saw George's sympathetic, somber eyes, she knew what he'd come to tell her. Tara tilted her head to one side and looked at him with quiet despair. "McGee's dead," she whispered. He nodded and stepped inside.

She crossed off the last name on her list of McGee's friends and sat staring at the phone in her lap. She felt as if she'd done nothing for the past two days but repeat George's information mechanically. The Shiites had announced that McGee and several other kidnap victims had recently been executed.

McGee was dead. That was the incontrovertible truth. And though she hadn't loved him for a long, long time, she grieved. In many ways he had been a wonderful man, and she had wished him only the best. Tara started to get up, then decided it wasn't worth the effort. Daylight was fading around the curtains in her bedroom, and her energy faded with it. She had nothing now, and she accepted that. Her life seemed as purposeless as the flight of a leaf caught in a storm. She knew that enthusiasm would return eventually, but for now she had no urge to give herself pep talks. Apathy was blessed relief, in a way.

The door chimes rang. Tara turned her head toward the sound lethargically. How had Bill let someone get past him downstairs? Perhaps it was another of her neighbors, coming to offer sympathy. She couldn't take more of that. Tara decided to ignore the visitor. The chimes sounded again, and she felt her back muscles tense with annoyance. I just want to be left alone! she thought angrily. Go the hell away!

Whoever was at the door began to knock loudly, quickly, stubbornly. Tara sighed and shook her head. Anger faded back to numbness. She stood slowly, brushed her hands distractedly across her loose white jogging suit and left the room. The fervent knocking continued as she crossed the living room unhurriedly. Frowning, Tara leaned her forehead against the door.

"Who's there, please?"

The pounding stopped. "Ethan," a deep, unmistakable voice answered.

Nine

She looked up at him unemotionally, and some still-functioning part of her mind noted that he was studying her with a deeply worried expression on his face. He wore no coat or tie. The sleeves of his white dress shirt were rolled up, and the collar was undone. His black trousers looked rumpled. His life had been as rough as hers, Tara thought.

"I heard about McGee," he told her.

"I'm not surprised. It's been in all the papers." She stepped back and nodded toward the living room. "Come in." His eyes never left her face as he stepped past her. She shut the door and simply stood, gazing at him dully. "McGee had no family. So I, as the ex-girlfriend, am getting a boatload of sympathy. I don't need any more."

Frowning, he brushed an errant strand of her dark, disheveled hair away from her face. Tara never moved, never even blinked. She didn't want his pity. She turned away and walked to the recliner, sat down slowly and waited, her hands clasped in her lap. The lines that accented his mouth deepened with displeasure as he watched her.

What do I do now? Ethan asked himself grimly. He couldn't bear to leave her alone, but it was obvious that she didn't give a damn that he was there.

"I want to help you," he told her. She shook her head slightly.

"I'm all right."

Her eyes were rimmed with the evidence of sleepless nights. Her sturdy, beautiful face was gaunt, and her bare feet looked frail, blue veins crisscrossing the tops. The love and anguish that had churned inside him for days exploded in anger. "Dammit, Tara, you're not all right! You look like hell!"

"Why, thank you," she said drolly. "That makes me feel much better."

He twisted to survey the living room. Pillows and blankets lay on the floor as if she'd been sleeping in front of the television set. An ashtray on the coffee table was crammed with cigarette butts. The place had a musty, closed-up smell. "What have you been doing for the past two weeks?"

"Existing, Ethan. And doing all right at it. I may look like hell, but I'm not a wilting flower." There was no rebuke in her voice, no plea for sympathy, no self-pity. There was no emotion at all, and it frightened him. He walked over to her, grasped her chin in one hand and tilted her face up for a shrewd inspection. He saw that her eyes were cloudy with fatigue.

"Thank you for defending me on *Nightline*," she said politely. "I appreciated that."

She doesn't love me, Ethan thought with grim sorrow. She needs me in so many ways, but she doesn't love me. And he knew now, even more than before, that he loved her desperately. That knowledge had driven him to go there, when he should never have risked being seen near her. It had driven him to pace the floor of his bedroom every night since they'd parted, aching for her smile and her touch. It drove him now to adopt a merciless facade that would hide his grief.

"Get up," he commanded her. "You're coming with me."

She registered no more emotion than before. "No."

"Get up!" He grabbed her harshly by the shoulders and hauled her to her feet. She gasped weakly and clung to his wrists. Ethan glared down at her, his stomach knotting. "Get some clothes. I'm taking you to my house."

"That's a very foolish offer."

"Dammit, don't analyze me!"

"What do you want from me?"

Seething with frustration because she was making it so difficult for him to take care of her, he retorted sarcastically, "You said that to make up for the trouble you'd caused, you'd do whatever I wanted you to do. I'm going to take advantage of your guilt."

Shock filtered into her gaze, and he was glad to see it, to see *anything* other than apathy.

"Ethan, does dominating me satisfy your need for revenge?"

"Yes," he breathed fiercely.

"Do you want us to sleep together?"

Ethan forced himself not to wince at what he had to say next. He'd do whatever was necessary to get her away from the lonely hell she'd created there. "Yes," he told her. "If sex is all you've got to offer, I'll take it."

After a moment's grim consideration, she nodded. "I'll honor that, then."

Damn her! he thought wretchedly. Could she reduce what they'd had, what they still had, to a debt of honor that her principles wouldn't let her ignore? All right, then, all right.

"Good," he told her curtly. "I'm sure you can imagine how rough my days have been lately. I want a distraction when I come home at night. No demands, no guilt, no talking about the mess we're both in. Just—''

"Good sex," she interjected wearily. "Just something to help you relax."

"That's right." He gave her a sardonic look. "And otherwise I'll leave you alone. During the day you'll have the run of the house. I have a cook who'll force-feed you as soon as she sees how thin you are. There's a pool and game room that will keep you entertained." He paused. "But you won't be able to leave the grounds, because the last thing I need is for someone from Logan to find out that you're staying with me."

"I understand. Let me pack a few things." She gently pushed his hands away and walked past him, headed toward her bedroom. She held herself proudly and moved with dutiful resolve. It nearly broke his heart.

Magnificent. His house suited him, Tara thought as she surveyed the landscaped backyard and oversized pool. He had switched on the exterior lights so that she could wander about. Ethan was closeted in his upstairs office, returning calls that his answering service had given him. She walked along a garden path bordered by waist-high azaleas, her hands sunk into the pockets of her jogging pants. Artistically placed lights threw pools of light across her sandaled feet.

She sat down on a wooden bench that had ornate wrought-iron legs and trim. Tara listened to the yard's huge oaks whisper in the spring darkness and gazed at the back of Ethan's house. It resembled an English cottage—only, no cottage had several levels containing four huge bedrooms, a library, a gym and a garden room with a redwood Jacuzzi.

The pool glittered like blue china in the outside lights. The redwood decks and cobblestone apron around it made an inviting area, with manicured ficus trees in large stone pots and an array of colorful deck furniture. Tara twisted her head and studied the backyard again, estimating that Ethan's home sat on at least two acres, possibly three. It appeared to be one of the most impressive estates in an impressive suburban community.

When she heard the double doors of the garden room swing open, she slowly turned her head to watch Ethan step onto the uppermost deck. He searched for her anxiously in the darkness beyond the pool, and she noted the subtle relaxing of his big body when he spotted her.

Despite what he'd said, he hadn't brought her there entirely for selfish satisfaction, she thought with a vague sense of tenderness. Had she really thought that he wanted them together again simply so that he could torment her, she would never have come. But for now, they would play the cynical, awkward game and she would ask for nothing except to be near him. Under her apathy lay the desperate hope that she could make him forget the problems the *Constitution*'s exposé had caused.

She stood and walked calmly toward him. He waited at the top of the decks, his expression carefully neutral, though his body radiated tension. They had hardly spoken a word during the long drive there, and he'd made only a pretense of conversation as he'd shown her around the house.

Tara stopped on the deck just below his and looked up at him somberly. "What now?" she asked.

His mouth thinned at her compliant, unconcerned tone. "I ran a tub of hot water for you in my bathroom. Go up and soak. I'll fix you some dinner."

"All right." She walked past him without another word and went into the house.

The master suite was as large as her condominium. Its ambiance was extremely masculine—warm, paneled walls, plush leather chairs, brass-and-stained-glass lamps and paintings of Western scenes. The suite consisted of his bedroom, a small office, a sitting room that doubled as a private library, and a huge bathroom with a sunken whirlpool tub and a skylight.

Tara closed her eyes and sank into the bubbling water, her hair catching in one of the lush plants that bordered the tub on three sides. The heat and the undulating rhythm of the water were irresistible, and for the first time in many days she fell asleep easily, her arms floating over her stomach.

She woke to the feeling of Ethan's blunt fingertips massaging her shoulders. As her eyes fluttered open, Tara whimpered with involuntary appreciation. Immediately he cupped her face with his warm hands, and she found herself looking up into his pensive eyes. He was kneeling on the floor, wearing nothing but a pair of black pajama bottoms. Apathy began to desert her, and she blinked back bittersweet tears.

For just one second his eyes softened into a look so gentle that she felt its heat in her soul. Then he dropped his hands from her face and sat back, his expression once again reserved.

"Your dinner is ready." With that, he got up and snapped a thick, white robe off the vanity, then stood above her, holding the robe open expectantly.

Tara felt her cheeks grow hot with embarrassment. During the magical weekend at her home, she had loved showing him her body. But then he'd looked at her with devotion and friendly delight, and now he looked with a coldly impatient attitude. She stepped out of the tub, vividly aware that water dripped from her jiggling breasts and ran in rivulets to the dark hair between her thighs. She turned her back and quickly slipped her arms into the robe's sleeves. The garment was huge, obviously his, and when he wrapped his arms around her to tie the belt, she shivered.

Ethan felt her body shake. He let go of her and walked out of the bathroom, his chest aching and heavy. She didn't want him to touch her, he thought bitterly.

He lay on the far side of his king-sized bed and read some office papers while she ate. Tara was propped up on pillows, a wicker lap tray across her legs. She ate mechanically, hardly tasting the rich shrimp salad, croissants and white wine he'd brought her. The room was shadowy and intimate; the satiny, darkly patterned bedspread seemed to weigh her legs down. She had no idea what to expect next from him, and she realized abruptly that she was afraid. If he touched her tonight in his cold, harsh mood, she would wither from sadness.

"I'm finished eating," she said, her heart thudding painfully. "I'll take this down to the kitchen."

"No." He came to her side of the bed and carried the tray to a heavy walnut dresser in one corner. "My housekeeper will get it in the morning." Ethan walked back to the bed and stopped beside her, gazing down with an unfathomable expression. "Her name is Samantha Powers. You should call her by her first name and expect the same in return. She stays at the house all day, but she won't pester you. Anything you need, just ask her. By the way, she cooks incredible pasta dishes and desserts. I want you to eat as much as you possibly can."

"Yes, *sir*," Tara answered with a hint of her old spirit. "I assume that Samantha is blithely accustomed to serving your live-in ladies?"

"No," he said in a sharp tone. "She's not accustomed to it at all. That's why she'll give you special treatment." He hesitated, his jaw working tensely. "I called her a little while ago and explained that she's not to discuss your presence here with anyone."

"You're embarrassed to have me here."

After an incredulous moment he answered in a low, taut voice, "I'm trying to salvage what I can of my credibility with the board of directors at Logan, and at the same time I'm harboring the woman who's directly responsible for the whole fiasco. If anyone finds that out, I'll look like a fool.

And the board would undoubtedly do what it's been on the verge of doing ever since the article ran in the *Constitution*—kick me out. I have important goals that would be blown to hell if that happened."

Tara clutched his robe to her body and shoved the covers down. Her voice was matter-of-fact. "It *is* ridiculous for you to take this risk. As things stand now, you'll never forgive my mistake. If you lost your position, you'd hate me. And I don't want that. I think I'll do us both a favor and leave."

His hand shot out and he grasped her shoulder, holding her still. Tara gazed up into blue eyes that had gone frigid. "If I want to be a fool, it's my business," he rasped. "You owe me a debt of honor. I want it paid." He held out his other hand. "Give me that robe and get back under the covers."

Her breath coming short, Tara shrugged the robe off and pulled it from around her. He turned on his heel and threw it across the room viciously. Feeling exposed and vulnerable, Tara pulled the covers over her and arranged the pillows for the night. He strode back to his side of the bed, his broad chest moving in a tight, quick rhythm. He snapped the bedside lamp off, and inky darkness closed around them.

Tara couldn't see a thing, but she could hear Ethan settle into bed and yank the covers over his body. At least, she thought ruefully, he'd chased away her apathy. Her skin grew clammy, and she began to tremble with dread.

His deep, Southern voice cut through the blackness. "Come over *here*," he said curtly.

Tara closed her eyes in grim shock. Ethan *was* going to torment her. She sensed that he wanted to break down the barriers between them as much as she did, and this wretched intimacy was the quickest way to do it. Trying to keep her teeth from chattering, she slid over to him. She prayed that the sad thing they were about to do would bring them both some measure of peace.

He was lying on his side. His arms surrounded her without gentleness, making her face him, and she winced as her breasts flattened against his naked torso. Her cheek rested against the curly hair on his chest, and she heard the harsh rhythm of his heart. Her abdomen brushed the silky material of his pajamas, and her thighs were forced into contact with his.

Tara recoiled when she found that he wasn't ready to make love, and her yielding attitude died.

"I can't..." she whispered raggedly, her hands bracing against his chest. "Not tonight. Not like this."

"Be still," he commanded her.

"I can't, Ethan." Crying now, she struggled to get away from him, but his long arms snaked farther around her. She heard his ragged breathing as his hands sought a tighter hold on her back. "Please let go of me. Please don't make me do this!"

"Give me a chance!" His voice sounded desperate and fierce. "Don't push me away!"

She tried to draw her knees up, like a barricade. He reached between their bodies and firmly shoved them down, then roughly jerked her to him again. "It won't be making love!" she begged. "It won't even be good sex!"

"Dammit! Who said anything about sex! I just want to hold you!" His voice sounded as if it might break. "Can't I just *hold* you? Have things changed between us so much that you don't even want *that*?"

Stunned, she stopped fighting him and lay quiet. The darkness was punctuated by the mingled sounds of their breathing. He cursed wearily and let go of her. As he started to move away, Tara realized that he was trembling as hard as she was. "Oh, Ethan," she said in a hoarse, tender voice. Her arms went around his neck and she clung to him. "I'd *love* for you to just hold me."

Ethan was amazed. After an incredulous moment, he groaned softly and put one hand on the back of her head, caressing her thick, tangled hair. "So you still need me."

"I wouldn't be here if I didn't."

"I thought . . . you were honoring your damned *duty*—"

"Yes. That's right." She lifted her head and kissed him. "But my duty is to make everything good between us again. I know it won't be easy."

"Shhh." His voice was throaty with emotion. "At least we're on the right track."

With a convulsive movement, he wrapped her deeply in his arms and slid one long leg between her thighs. They were two brilliantly burning suns in an unfriendly universe, but now they could fight the darkness as one.

"Go to sleep," he urged her in a raspy whisper. "And maybe tomorrow we'll be able to make sense out of what's happening to us. For right now, all that matters is that you're with me."

"I'm *glad* to be with you, Ethan."

He hugged her tightly, and neither of them spoke again. They both knew that their problems were far from over, but they let the silence pretend.

He kissed her goodbye before dawn and warned her that Samantha would let him know if Tara didn't sleep late. She did, and spent the remainder of the day at a table by the pool, eating almost constantly—thanks to the smiling, motherly Samantha—and working up a list of job leads.

Ethan didn't return until after dinner, and she knew from his quiet aura of tension that his day had been exceptionally bad, full of struggles to regain his control at Logan. Hurting and depressed, Tara made herself keep silent when he secluded himself in the den downstairs with a briefcase full of paperwork. She retreated to the library in the master suite and read a novel until past midnight. Restlessness and worry finally got the better of her, and she went downstairs. She tapped at the den's door.

"Come in," he said brusquely.

He sat at a teakwood desk in one corner, paperwork scattered under the light of a single Tiffany lamp, his face etched with fatigue. His tan slacks and white polo shirt were rumpled. He was barefoot, and his blond hair was disheveled. He glanced up, his expression guarded, and studied her. Tara abruptly wished that she'd put a robe over her lacy white teddy. The frown that crossed his face told her that he thought she was deliberately trying to distract him.

"May I sit down for a moment?" she asked politely. He nodded, and she went to the brown leather couch that faced his desk. Tara settled on it and nervously pretended to gaze at the room's walls, where classics in Old West art were displayed. The collection was a personal hobby of Ethan's, Samantha had explained. There are so many things I still need to learn about him, Tara thought sadly. And he's shutting me out.

"Can't sleep?" he asked. "Don't wait for me."

"Is there anything I can do? Can I fix you something to eat? Or rub your back? Or—"

"No," he retorted. "There's nothing."

Tara gave him a wistful look. "I've already done enough, I suppose," she said in a soft, neutral tone. "Too much." She meant the Logan problem, and he knew it. Tara lifted her chin proudly. "If you've changed your mind about wanting me here—"

"Dammit, we settled that discussion last night. I don't have the time or energy to go through it again. I *want* you here. Now, go to bed, please."

She stood up stiffly. After a moment's consideration she decided she couldn't leave the room without making some kind of tender connection with him. Tara went to the desk, bent over and kissed him gently on the mouth. When she drew back, she saw the bittersweet look in his eyes and knew that she'd done the right thing. "If you need a friend, I'll be upstairs," she told him.

She was almost to the couch when she heard his chair scrape back roughly. "Wait. Tara, *wait*." She turned around to watch him coming toward her, his expression full of sorrow and self-rebuke. The pleading look in his eyes weakened her knees, and she sank onto the couch again. He knelt beside her and took her face between his hands. She slid gentle fingers around his wrists and tilted her head back to look at him.

"I'm sorry. I'm being a bastard," he murmured. "And you don't deserve it."

"Shhh. I got you into this mess."

"It doesn't matter."

"It *does* matter, Ethan. My mistake will always be between us. And there's nothing I can do to change it. That makes me miserable."

"I don't want you to be miserable," he protested. He put his head on her shoulder and took her in his arms. "My beautiful Tara. For two cents I'd tell everyone to go to hell and we'd run off to an island somewhere."

"Please let me make you feel better. Please. If only for a few minutes." She twisted her face to his and kissed him wantonly. He groaned into her vulnerable, pleading mouth. Something desperate ignited between them, and he pushed her down on the couch, his body grinding against hers. His sudden passion was rough and demanding, a mindless urge to destroy pain with pleasure, and she returned it.

They bruised each other with harsh kisses and arched their bodies desperately, seeking sensation through their clothes. Ethan twisted one hand into the silky white material between her legs and opened the snaps of the teddy. Tara jerked the fastenings on his trousers open and coaxed him with caresses that made his hips move against her.

She cried out when Ethan plunged inside her, but the sensation was sweeter for being so wild. His loud groans and deep, impatient thrusts took her further than ever before, and just when she thought she could spiral no higher, she did. Tara muffled a high-pitched sound against his neck and then writhed out of control. He pulled back, his half-shut eyes riveted on her. Tara's heels dug into his legs as Ethan raised her hips to meet his final, shuddering stroke.

They lay joined for a long time afterward, their hands feathering over each other in gentle contrast to the fierceness of before. The peaceful interlude made them drowsy, and Tara stroked his back until she heard his breathing become soft and even against her ear. She fell asleep under him, her arms draped loosely around his neck. When they woke up an hour later, he asked her to stay with him while he continued working. Tara got a blanket and lay on the couch, watching him, watching over him, and wishing that the night would never end.

"She resigned from her job, Ethan," Maggie Logan repeated in her husky voice. She stood at the huge windows of his office, staring grimly over the New York cityscape. "I suspected as much, but I had to check with my, um, private sources at the newspaper before I butted in. She wasn't fired. When they told her that they wouldn't honor the confidentiality of her notes on you, she told them to go to hell and *resigned*."

Behind her, Ethan still stood in stunned silence. Dear God, could Tara have done that if she didn't love me? And then remorse began to tear him apart. She'd sacrificed everything she could for him, he thought. And then she'd suffered in silence so that he could indulge in bitterness.

Maggie turned toward him and put her hands on her hips. Her attitude was commanding. "I hope you appreciate the fact that she absolutely adores you."

He arched a brow at her tone of voice. Because of his closeness to Killihan Logan, he had known Maggie for

years. She was the only woman in the world who treated him
like an errant older brother in need of scolding.

"I do."

"And what are you going to do about it?"

Ethan pushed the intercom button on his phone console.
"Dora?"

"Yes, sir?"

"I'm going home to take care of a personal emergency.
Call down for my car. And forward my messages."

"Why... yes, sir."

After he turned the intercom off, he glanced up to find
Maggie smiling at him wryly, her head tilted. "I want an
invitation to the wedding."

The floating pool chair was deliciously comfortable. Half
dozing behind dark sunglasses, Tara tried to let the heat of
the June sun coax her tensions away. But too many questions whirled in her mind, and she shifted restlessly, lolling
her head from one side to the other.

Harsh thoughts tormented her. Would Ethan's feelings
for her slowly disintegrate under the awful strain of his
power struggle at Logan? What *did* he feel for her? She was
thirty years old, and he was nearing forty. Did maturity
dictate that they shouldn't say "I love you" until they had
known each other for a long time? Both of us... old bachelors, she considered groggily. I... don't want to be... does
he? His biological options were different from hers, because he could wait many years to settle down with someone and start a family.

Tara pictured Ethan at sixty, distinguished, still a heart-
stopper. Young women would be eager to marry him. Tara
pulled her sunglasses off, threw them in her lap and covered her face with both hands. She was going to lose him,
she thought in a rush of despair.

A loud splashing sound coincided with a wave that nearly
turned her pool chair over. Tara gasped and looked around

frantically. Intruder? she thought. Samantha? Her pool chair careened again as two brawny hands rose from underneath to grip its side. Tara screamed as the hands flipped it over. She plunged blindly into the water and came up soaked, kicking, sputtering, and in Ethan's arms.

Water matted his golden hair to his head and traced paths in the thick hair on his chest. He smiled down at her rakishly and let his eyes roam over her black maillot.

"What are you doing here at this time of day?" she demanded, amazed. Why did he look so happy? she added silently.

"I came home to make love to you in the swimming pool."

"Does Samantha know about this?"

"I sent her home early."

Something nudged her from underneath. Tara gasped. "You're naked!"

"The best way to be, don't you think? In a minute you're going to be naked, too." He set her down, turned her to face him and cupped her face in his hands. His lighthearted expression faded and was replaced by a look of searing, sweet devotion that made her bones melt. "But first I have something to say."

"Ethan, what's happened, why are you—"

"I *love* you," he whispered. "I've loved you for a long time, but I didn't know if you wanted to hear me say it. Now I think that you do. I *hope* that you do."

Tara gazed up at him in wonder. "I do," she whispered back.

His blue eyes seemed to turn several shades darker as they filled with even more happiness. "I like I-do's," he told her in a husky tone. "I intend to ask for more of them."

The implication was so overwhelming that she sagged against him, her hands sliding weakly up his chest for support. He held her closer and searched her face. "Do *you* love me?" he asked.

"Oh, yes," she nearly groaned. "I love you dearly."

He gave her a slow, blissful smile. "Then you've just made everything right between us again."

Ten

——

"Ethan! Deer!"

"You're dear yourself," he mumbled sleepily. "Come back to bed."

"No, the four-footed kind of deer! There's one outside, nibbling leaves off a bush!" Tara, seated at a low, open window, was enchanted by the delicate creature, which was eating a dewy breakfast in the rose-colored light of an August dawn.

"Deer do that sort of thing," Ethan yawned. "They like salads."

Exasperated, Tara crept across the floor of his rugged Kentucky cabin to the big pine-log bed in one corner. Ethan lay on his back, his eyes closed peacefully, his arms over his head, a white sheet slung low across his abdomen. She grasped a tuft of his chest hair and tugged fiendishly.

"Ouch!" He grabbed her by one wrist and pulled her across his body, then slapped her bottom.

Laughing, she ducked her head and bit his side. They wrestled playfully for a minute and ended in a tangle of legs and arms, the sheet on the floor. Tara grinned at him. "Good morning."

"Good morning." He kissed the tip of her nose. "Haven't you ever seen a deer before?"

"Not outside a zoo."

"Well, you're in the middle of eastern Kentucky, now. You might even see a bear."

"Not if I can help it." She snuggled into the crook of his shoulder and sighed contentedly. "Except for bears, I like this place."

"I thought you might. I haven't come here in months, and I've had an itch to get back. This is where I come when I really need to escape."

"I needed a vacation, too. This is wonderful, even if it's just a long weekend."

A month ago she'd gone to work for Affiliated Press Worldwide, one of the major wire services. It was a good position—staff medical writer in APW's New York office—but demanding. She intended to relax during this weekend at Ethan's mountain hideaway, and she was going to make certain that he relaxed, too. Though he avoided discussing problems at Logan, because they depressed her and brought back her guilt, Tara knew that his corporate life continued to be stressful.

Everything he did was questioned now. The board of directors was evenly divided—half willing to trust him with the company's future, half skeptical. He was trapped in a tug-of-war between the factions and played a masterful game of corporate politics that often left him exhausted and worried.

But for this weekend, at least, the two of them were alone in a magnificent world of rolling green mountains and incredible views. The cabin sat atop a ridge, surrounded by rhododendron and hardwoods, a stream curving down the hill in front of it. The nearest paved road was two miles away, connected to them by only a narrow logging road. They'd driven there in a Jeep.

"Rub my back," Ethan asked in mock command. Then he turned over and stretched languorously, like a tawny lion. Tara swept a wicked gaze over his bare rump and long, powerful legs, then smiled with gentle rebuke. The man knew that she was watching every muscle flex in that fantastic body.

"Yes, m'lord." She straddled his hips and began to massage.

"Ah, a cheerful wench, and eager to serve."

"Because I want you to enjoy this, I'm not going to pinch your fanny."

"A wise move, girl. Pleasure me, and I'll pleasure thee in return, anon."

"You *bet* you will."

And he did, beautifully, making love to her until long after the sun had climbed above the eastern horizon and sent light cascading through the cabin's screen door. They fixed a huge breakfast, and she ate grits for the first time in her life. She liked them, though she made him laugh by insisting that they ought to be eaten with milk and sugar.

"Listen, Yankee, the only *legal* things you can put on grits are salt, pepper, butter and red-eye gravy," he told her. "Although it is permissible to stir the yoke of your fried egg into them, if you insist."

"Ugh. Gooey egg yoke and grits. I wouldn't know whether to eat it or give it a decent funeral."

After breakfast they packed a knapsack with cheese, crackers, pickles and a thermos of iced tea, and spent the day hiking. Tara carried her camera, one that made instant photographs, and tried in vain to capture the majesty of the land.

They stopped for lunch in a glen bounded by mountains on every side. Because the weather was baking hot, they lay down on their backs with their bare feet in the edge of a tiny creek. They were companionably silent for a while, studying the clouds that floated in a deep blue sky. "Mae West," he said, pointing to one.

"Nah. It's a Volkswagen."

"We'll go outside tonight and look at the constellations. You can't argue about those."

She laughed. "I yield to your expertise about astronomy, but not to your claims about cloud formations." Tara thought for a moment, and her voice became pensive. "I think you ought to go back to college someday and study astronomy, the way you wanted to years ago."

"I doubt I'll ever have time."

"Maybe . . . maybe you'll leave Logan eventually."

"I doubt it."

Tara rose on her elbow and turned to look at him. His eyes were somber. "Not ever?" she asked in surprise. "Even if you can't accomplish the goals you set for the company? I mean, if you can't get Logan out of the tobacco business?"

"I don't want to give up on the company."

"Ethan," she said in gentle rebuke. Tara feathered her fingers across his hair. "Do you ever wonder if you're fighting a losing battle?" She grimaced. "Even before I threw a monkey wrench in your plans?"

"Shhh. The article in the *Constitution* just provoked confrontations that would have come eventually, anyway." His eyes filled with dismay. "I expect support from you, not doubts."

Tara shoved his shoulder lightly and arched a brow at him. "I *do* support you. I believe in you and I trust you, and I love you for what you're trying to do at Logan."

His subtle tension faded, and he smiled at her wearily. "You make me feel heroic. I'm not. I'm just tenacious and stubborn."

"And loyal and idealistic—"

"No. Practical. I'm trying to do what's best for Logan, which is to get it out of the tobacco business."

"Have it your way. I hate to think how surprised you're going to be when you realize one day that you have scruples."

He laughed ruefully and sidestepped the subject. "If we lie here much longer, I'm going to realize that I have chigger bites."

Tara sighed, knowing it was pointless to continue their discussion. She kissed him tenderly and pillowed her head on his shoulder, her eyes troubled. As she had done many times over the past weeks, she considered how the Logan board members would react if they ever found out about her and Ethan. The tobacco would hit the fan, she thought grimly.

Though she and Ethan never discussed the need for secrecy, their relationship was bound by it. They stayed away from public gatherings where they might be seen together by someone from Logan. He couldn't introduce her to his friends and she couldn't introduce him to hers, for fear that word would travel. But the board would find out about them someday, Tara thought. It was inevitable. What would Ethan do then?

Ethan was laughing as Tara unlocked the door to her condominium. "And so Eva says to Eddie Albert," he continued as they entered the living room and tossed their tote bags on the couch, "'But darleeng, Mr. Ziffle tinks of Arnold as his son. Shouldn't his son go to college, even if he eez a peeg?'"

"Enough already, enough," Tara protested, chuckling. She switched on the floor lamp. "I promise not to tell *you* any more Three Stooges stories if you promise not to quote *me* dialogue from *Green Acres*."

"Checkmate," he agreed.

They put their arms around each other and hugged bois-
terously. "Good weekend," Tara murmured into the solid
warmth of his shoulder. "I'm sorry it's over."

"That suit I left here. Have you gotten it back from the
cleaners yet?"

"Mm-hmm. And your shirt, too."

"Good. Then I don't have to go home tonight." He nuzzled her hair. "I can stay with you and leave for the office
from here in the morning."

"That's why I made certain that I had your clothes
ready." She squeezed his back lovingly.

He chuckled, pleased. "Scheming woman."

"You got it."

He whirled her around and then kissed her. "I'll make
dinner. How about some vegetables with Southern-fried
pork chops? And corn bread?"

"I'll have to run ten miles tomorrow to burn it all off."

Ethan smiled wickedly. "So? You'll need something to
keep you busy when you're alone tomorrow night. All that
bottled-up sexual tension..."

"I'd best run *twenty* miles."

They snickered and rubbed noses, Eskimo-style. "When
I'm alone, I get in my pool and make the water steam..."
he began just as the security intercom clicked on. They both
looked toward it.

"Ms. Ross?"

"Yes, Bill."

"Mr. Bennett from the State Department is here in the
lobby. Should I send him up?"

Tara frowned and withdrew from Ethan's embrace, her
heart rate accelerating. "Yes...thanks." She looked up at
Ethan anxiously, and her voice grew husky with sadness. "It
must be about McGee."

He touched her arm, offering gentle support. "They've
probably found his body."

Tara nodded, sorrow and dread settling in the pit of her stomach. Ethan gestured toward the bedroom. "Would it be best if I disappear while Bennett's here?"

"No." She grasped his hand. "I need you."

They stood there, waiting, until the door chimes sounded a moment later. Tara moved forward stiffly, her body already building defenses against George's announcement. But when she opened the door, she found him grinning at her. Tara caught her breath and pressed both hands to her mouth.

"He's alive," George told her gleefully. "And he's coming home."

She screamed with delight and threw her arms around George's neck. Behind her, Ethan stood in stunned shock, watching.

The small waiting room at the London airport was cool, but Tara's face burned with nervousness. She shifted from one foot to the other, then paced, her hands clasped behind her. How do I look? she asked herself for the tenth time. She glanced down at her cotton twill dress, hoping that its soft burgundy plaid wouldn't make her appear too somber. She hadn't wanted to look seductive, but perhaps she'd gone too far in the opposite direction.

Tara sat down on a green vinyl couch in one corner, then immediately got back up, too restless to be still. A great part of her uneasiness had to do with Ethan. He'd seen her off in New York, and he'd done a magnificent job of being supportive and cheerful. He understood why she'd had to go there today to meet McGee, she assured herself. Ethan knew that she needed to help McGee for reasons that had nothing to do with romantic love. But still, there had been something in Ethan's blue eyes . . . a sort of stoic look that hinted at concern. Dear man, she told him now silently, how could I ever love anyone but you? Don't worry.

A knock sounded at the waiting room door, and Tara swung around, her eyes wide. "Come in."

The door was pushed open by a British military official of some undeterminable rank. He winked at her and held the door wide, then looked over his shoulder and gestured for someone to enter. From the sounds in the hallway, Tara knew that a crowd of people were waiting.

But only one of them walked into the room. He stopped just inside, and the official departed, closing the door softly. The man was tall and pitifully thin, much too thin for the green military fatigues he wore. His thick brown hair needed a barber's attention, and his complexion had an unhealthy pallor to it. But his gray eyes gleamed with indomitable spirit and pure happiness.

"Rossy," he said in a soft, husky voice. Tears slipped down to his crooked, teasing smile. "My God, Rossy. We've got to stop meeting like this." Tara laughed, but tears pooled in her own eyes. McGee would always be outrageous, and she would always want to be his friend. She ran to him and threw her arms around his neck.

He hugged her weakly and buried his head against her shoulder. "Oh, Rossy," he whispered in a hoarse tone, "I knew you'd be waiting."

"This is Amanda Christopher. Mr. Boone is expecting my call."

"Indeed," Dora Brown said gruffly. "Please hold."

Tara sighed, the phone clutched tightly to her ear. Good old Dora knows exactly who I am, she thought. The woman had never been fooled by the alias. Tara had mentioned that suspicion to Ethan once, and he'd confirmed it. But Mrs. Brown, for all her icy reserve, was as loyal as a mother.

"Hi," Ethan said in a moment. "You're back?"

"I'm back. I'm at the condo."

"How is McGee?"

"Thin. Exhausted. A little disoriented and numb, but the doctors say that's normal. In fact, they say he's in good shape for a man who's been through hell for two years."

"Have you seen the *Constitution*'s front page?"

"Not yet."

"They're calling him a hero. My God, he *is* a hero. No wonder the Shiites wanted everyone to think he'd been executed. Not many kidnap victims manage to kill two of their guards and escape. Did he really hide in a brothel until he could meet with a trustworthy Syrian official?"

Tara chuckled ruefully. "Mm-hmm. Ever the dedicated cameraman, McGee says that he was gathering background for a documentary. He's going to call it *Bad Girls of Beirut*. You'd have to know McGee to appreciate the humor."

"I want to meet him. Where's he staying?"

Tara drew a deep breath and shut her eyes. Please understand, sweetheart, she begged silently. "At my place."

The silence was frightening. "Why?" Ethan asked in a soft, strained voice.

"Because he has no family."

"You told me that he has friends all over the country. *Good* friends."

"Ethan . . . he can barely take care of himself. He needs help. The State Department was going to put him in a hotel room here. I took him to it, and he sat down on the bed, and he just looked . . . lost. I couldn't stand it."

"All right." He paused, composing a good-natured facade. "I'm the last person in the world who should be surprised at your sense of duty to McGee. I love you for caring about him." He cleared his throat. "Bring him to *my* house, and Samantha will go berserk with motherliness."

Tara smiled as a sweet sense of adoration filled her. How many men would be willing to host their lady's ex-lover? She knew, of course, that Ethan was fighting a battle between

jealousy and common sense, but that didn't make his offer
less endearing.

"Ethan," she rebuked gently, "McGee is a celebrity.
Everyone would know that he's staying at your home. And
it's no secret that he and I used to be involved. How could
you explain the connection to your board?"

"I'm a helluva good samaritan? Patriotic—"

"You're wonderful, and I love you. But you can't do it."

He sighed in defeat. "He's staying in the guest room?"

"Hmm."

"Evasive maneuvers aren't your strong suit, honey. Just
admit that you've given him the main bedroom." Tara could
almost read his thoughts. Our bedroom, he was musing.
Our bed.

"He needs the space, Ethan. The man's got a permanent
case of claustrophobia."

"Let's take him out to dinner, then. Every night I'll come
over, and we'll take him out to dinner."

"You can't be seen with McGee and me."

"Dammit," he said softly, agreeing but unhappy. His
frustration over their secret relationship was near the boil-
ing point.

Tara rested her forehead in one hand. She was hurting
Ethan so badly, and there was nothing she could do about
it. "I haven't told him about you," she murmured.

"An oversight I want you to rectify immediately," he said
jauntily.

She spoke in a soothing but firm voice. "Ethan, do you
trust me?"

"Yes."

"Then you know you shouldn't feel threatened by
McGee."

"If *I* hadn't seen you for two years, I wouldn't want to
sleep alone in your bed. The sooner you explain about us,
the better it will be for McGee . . . and me."

"McGee doesn't expect anything but friendship. He knows that our...romantic situation...isn't any different now than when he left for Lebanon."

Ethan's voice rose as he said, "He doesn't know a damned thing except that you're still single, living alone and desperate to play nurse to him!"

"Oh, Ethan, stop it!"

He spoke between clenched teeth. "Tell...him... about...me."

"He's just gotten home, Ethan! He's confused and depressed and all alone except for me! What am I going to do? March up to him and say, 'Look, McGee, it's a big sacrifice for me to keep you here, because my new friend's furious about it'? I *will* tell him about us, as soon as he's gotten his life stabilized a little."

"I hurt for the guy, I really do. I don't mean to sound selfish. But I *envy* him. When can I see you?"

"I don't know," she said in a small, tormented voice. "But I'd give anything to be with you right now, so that I could try to make you understand why I'm doing all of this."

"I understand," he said wearily. "But I don't know how long I can deal with it rationally. Hell, I don't think I'm dealing with it rationally now. I love you too much to just idly sit back and let McGee take over your life."

"Please be patient."

He chuckled in a strained, worried way that showed her how he strove desperately for lightness. "So what have you done with the clothes I left at your place? And my electric razor? Not to mention the...personal items...that we keep in the drawer beside the bed?"

"It's all in a cardboard box in my closet."

Deadly silence stretched across the phone line. "Marked 'disposable,' I assume."

"Oh, Ethan."

He was becoming angry again. "You have one week. One week, and then you've got to tell McGee about us."

She had forgotten how domineering Ethan could be and how much it provoked her when he was. "I don't know if that will be enough time."

"It'll have to be."

"No."

"It will *have* to be," he repeated curtly.

After they hung up, Tara sat brooding, her head in her hands. She glanced toward her bedroom, where McGee was asleep. Now that she was off the phone, she'd have to open the bedroom door. He'd specifically requested that she never shut it, because he often woke up with nightmares about being suffocated in a room where the walls moved inward lethally. She shook her head, tears for both Ethan and McGee burning her eyes. Ethan would *have* to be patient. The trauma she and he were suffering was nothing compared to what McGee had gone through.

He would never get Logan out of the tobacco business. Ethan knew that now, though he refused to let the knowledge crystallize in his thoughts. It lurked underneath, and he allowed his sense of defeat to surface only as a heavy feeling that weighed on his shoulders and an ache that soured in the pit of his stomach.

He scanned the faces around his table at Napoleon's, an elegant Manhattan restaurant. He was looking at the future of Logan Tobacco, he thought. Interspersed among Logan board members, the Chinese officials seemed culturally displaced in their black dinner jackets, but their jubilant expressions were purely Western. They knew that the Logan board was anxious to cooperate on a joint manufacturing venture in their country. The Chinese bought one *trillion* cigarettes a year, and despite all Ethan's efforts, Logan Tobacco was going to make sure that they bought even more.

Maggie, dressed in a glittering black evening gown, sat to his right. She's such a con artist, Ethan thought affectionately, watching her listen to one of their guests with apparent pleasure. She hated this as much as he did.

Ethan distractedly ran a hand across his snug black cummerbund, wishing he could take it off. Damned uncomfortable tuxedos, he thought grimly. He had a whole collection of them, custom-tailored, but not one he enjoyed wearing. To the rest of the people at this elegant, crystal-and-linen-set table, he knew that he appeared relaxed and attentive. His true feelings gnawed painfully inside him, making him clench his teeth. I need to see Tara, he thought. I need to talk to her. Dear God, I need to hear her voice. I need her. Nearly a week had passed since McGee's arrival.

With forced casualness, Ethan let his eyes stray from his companions. The Logan group was dining in a private gallery that overlooked the restaurant's main floor. Ethan gazed down at the haute-French decor and the tables of well-dressed diners. As he watched, people suddenly began to turn in their chairs, whispering excitedly and looking toward the entrance to the main floor. One of the male diners stood and called, "Bravo!" Others followed, applauding.

Who just walked in? Ethan wondered. He glanced at the people seated with him. Chinese dignitaries and Logan board members craned their heads in mutual curiosity, trying to see who had arrived to stir such interest among jaded New Yorkers.

"Perhaps we're going to be treated to a glance at one of our entertainment stars," Ethan told his group. The Chinese visitors registered immediate excitement.

"Liz Taylor?" one questioned in a fractured accent. "We would very much like to see Liz."

Ethan laughed politely and returned his gaze to the floor below them. Nearly everyone in the restaurant was standing now, whistling and applauding. A maître d' parted the sea of admiring people. Behind him, hand in hand, were Tara and McGee.

Ethan's chest tightened with a strangling mixture of jealousy and pride. Without thinking, he reached forward and gripped the gilded balustrade that bordered the gallery, his fingers digging into it as if they might rip the wood. She'd never looked more beautiful, he thought with a nearly physical ache of pleasure and pain.

She had somehow arranged her shoulder-length hair into a soft, upswept style that showed the graceful strength of her neck. She wore a white Victorian blouse and a floor-length gray skirt of some silky material. This is how she should be able to dress when she's with me, Ethan thought wretchedly. The secrecy of their relationship had never allowed them to attend any event that required formal clothes.

McGee Webster, on the other hand, looked like such a scarecrow that Ethan couldn't help feeling sympathy for him. His tuxedo did little to hide the emaciated condition of his tall body, and his face was so gaunt that his smile seemed ridiculously out of place.

Ethan dimly overheard Maggie explaining McGee's story to the Chinese. Look up, honey, he commanded Tara silently. I love you. Look up and smile at me. But she was obviously distracted by the crowd's response, and her actions were focused on getting the weak-looking McGee quickly through the crowd. When the two of them angled under the gallery to a table Ethan couldn't see, he sank back in his chair and rubbed his forehead wearily.

"...That woman...*she's* the one...Damned writer for the *Constitution*...They fired her after she screwed us over, you remember...." He heard Barkley Stewart, Logan's president, muttering to one of the board members. Ethan turned toward the two men with a killing glare that stunned them. They gave him startled, then quizzical, looks. Stewart leaned toward him so that the rest of the table couldn't hear.

"Personal problem, Ethan?"

"I don't want to hear you discuss Tara Ross in front of our guests," Ethan answered in a low, lethal voice. "This isn't the place. And for your information, she wasn't fired. She resigned."

"Why are *you* concerned about that woman's reputation?"

Ethan, his eyes narrowed, all diplomacy gone, whispered a few basic, brutal words that told Stewart to shut up. The man sat back, rigid with anger. Ethan, his fists clenched, smiled at him, then turned the smile toward the rest of the table.

"We Americans are very proud of McGee Webster," he told the Chinese. Ethan felt tension spreading among the board members, who were aware that some mysterious, volatile communication had just taken place between their two top executives.

The rest of the dinner seemed to take hours. Ethan felt the board members eyeing him. Maggie smiled at him, pleased at the trouble he'd started, because she loved to make the rest of the board members squirm. She was still smiling as they shepherded the group downstairs after dinner.

As soon as they reached the restaurant's chandeliered lobby, Ethan knew that some new excitement was stirring. The lobby was crowded, and people stood on tiptoe to gaze at a central point of interest. "Liz Taylor?" one of the Chinese officials asked hopefully.

Ethan was too busy looking for Tara to answer him. As the Logan group melded with the rest of the restaurant's patrons, he strained his eyes to see if McGee was again the focus of the attention. Ethan had a height advantage on most of the men in the lobby, and he finally located the trouble. His heart jerked.

McGee lay on the floor, his eyes shut. Tara knelt beside him, cupping his head in one hand. Other people bent beside her, offering advice but little help. She glanced up at them, and Ethan saw the desperate, worried look on her face. It was too much for him to bear. He began to shove his way toward her, ignoring Maggie's low, horrified "Ethan, don't be a fool!"

He reached Tara and McGee quickly. When she saw him, her green eyes filled with shock but also undeniable relief. Ethan knelt on the other side of McGee and reached across him, laying one hand alongside her face in a soothing caress. The adoration that slipped into her eyes destroyed his last thought of self-preservation. But she shook her head urgently.

"Go," she commanded in a hoarse, barely audible voice. "This is insane, for you to be here."

"He fainted?"

"Yes. He's all right. He warned me earlier that he was hyperventilating. Someone's gone to get a cool cloth." She glanced around worriedly, and her voice became more fervent. "Ethan! Get out of here!"

A waiter appeared with a damp towel, and Tara began dabbing McGee's pinched white face with it. His eyes flickered halfway open. "Rossy to the rescue," he murmured weakly, and tried to smile. A grimace replaced the attempt. "Sorry, kid, sorry."

"Can it," she teased him gruffly. "You love to show off, don't you?"

Ethan began loosening McGee's collar, but he kept watching Tara's face. He wasn't a man who frightened easily, but his stomach knotted in queasy dread at the affection and concern that she was showing another man. *She may not love him, but she cares about him deeply,* he thought in shock. *More than I ever realized.*

Ethan felt a hand grip his shoulder; Maggie's husky, tense voice rasped in his ear. "Tara can handle this alone! Stewart and the damned board members are watching this scene! Dammit, you *have* to leave, Ethan!"

"Yes," Tara agreed in a choking voice. "Go!"

Ethan looked into her anguished eyes and knew that his presence was only compounding her anxiety. He stood, his chest moving roughly, his jaw tight. McGee is her whole world, he acknowledged suddenly. And he needs her even worse than I do. And maybe she loves him but won't admit it.

She gave him a bittersweet look and started to say something, but McGee's soft groan distracted her. His throat burning, Ethan turned on his heel and pushed his way through the crowd. On the way out of the restaurant, he made diplomatic replies to the board members' hushed, angry inquiries. Ethan hardly knew what he was telling them, and didn't particularly care.

His thoughts stayed with Tara. A popular cliché, one he had always disdained in the past, kept ringing in his mind: *If you love something, set it free. If it comes back to you, you'll know that it's yours forever.* He silently, painfully set Tara free.

Eleven

Tara exited the revolving doors of the skyscraper that housed Affiliated Press Worldwide. She paused, gazing ruefully at the noontime crowd that packed the sidewalk. She started to work her way into the flow of people, then spotted the black stretch limousine parked at the curb. A familiar, uniformed driver straightened formally beside the back passenger door.

She walked toward him, smiling quizzically while a sense of foreboding made her pulse jump. Tara said lightly, "Why, hello, Sam. Are we going to lunch?"

He shook his head and looked at her somberly. "I'm taking Mr. Boone to the airport. He wants to meet with you for a moment."

The airport? she repeated silently, her lips parting in dismay. Of course, Ethan had to travel a great deal in his position with Logan, but something about Sam's expression told her that this trip was different. Sam opened the limousine's door and she slipped inside the cool, dark interior. As she faced Ethan, she dimly heard the door shut.

He looked reserved and forbidding, his face lined with fatigue and his blue eyes guarded. "Where have you been?" she said in a low, worried voice. "I've been trying to get in touch with you for three days." Tara slid toward him, eager to feel his arms around her, eager to pour out all her devotion for what he'd done at the restaurant. When he held up one hand, she froze, amazed.

"I'm leaving for China today," he told her. "Let's not make this any more difficult than it already is."

She gasped. His cool, authoritative tone would have hurt her deeply, had she not heard the undertone of sorrow in it. Tara raised one hand in supplication, but he shook his head. Stunned, she limply dropped the hand back into her lap and looked at him in astonishment.

"For how long?"

"Two weeks. Then I'll be going straight to the Logan plant in Kenya. After that, to Brazil. Our foreign markets."

An awful feeling of fear made goose bumps rise along her spine. "How long, altogether?" she asked numbly.

"Four weeks."

The announcement was like a blow. "Oh, *Ethan*. Why? You've never done anything like this before."

He shrugged lightly. "Business."

"Ethan...I..." Tara struggled to rid herself of the knot in her throat. For a moment she gazed at him in speechless despair. She needed him so badly, she wanted to say. Even if they couldn't be together, she needed to know that he was nearby. But those words would only make him feel worse. "We're going to have a heck of a telephone bill," she managed lightly.

He shook his head again. "You need this time alone with McGee, without distractions. I'm...not going to call you."

Depression and bewilderment coiled in her stomach. "What is it? What's wrong?"

"I don't regret trying to help you the other night. But now I'm fighting for my life at Logan, and it would be best if you and I didn't contact each other for a while."

Desperation nearly choked Tara's voice, as she said, "You don't have to seclude yourself in the far corners of the world! How can you think that will make anything better! Ethan—"

"I have business to take care of," he interrupted her.

"Ethan, don't do this!"

"It's business," he repeated in a strained voice. "I have to go."

"No!"

He reached forward suddenly and grasped her face between his hands. Tara saw the tears glittering in his eyes, and groaned.

"Goodbye," he whispered hoarsely. He bent his head to hers and gave her a deep, rough kiss.

Oh, God, how am I going to get through the next few weeks without her? he thought wretchedly. He tightened his fingers against Tara's face and tasted her vulnerable, open mouth again and again, nearly bruising her with his intensity. Tara made a soft, distressed sound in the back of her throat.

She knew only that Ethan was leaving her for an eternity, that he had retreated behind a frightening wall of resistance, that she had to do something unexpected and totally reckless to break that wall down. Her hands fierce, she quickly unbuttoned her blouse. He drew back, his face registering shock and then understanding.

"Don't," he rasped. He caught at her hands, trying to stop her, but she flung the blouse off.

Tara ground the words out: "We're in total privacy. No one can see us through the limo's windows—"

"Dammit, don't!"

But she pushed him away and hooked her fingers under the straps of her bra and slip. Tara jerked the garments down to her waist and looked at Ethan with urgent eyes. "Touch me," she ordered in a tearstained voice. "Please."

Agonized by the sight of her disheveled and defenseless, he shuddered. Concern for her tore his reserve apart. Ethan shut his eyes and exhaled harshly. "Oh, honey," he whispered like a plea for mercy, and pulled her into his lap.

One big hand rose to press her head into the crook of his neck. The other splayed on the center of her bare back, the fingers digging into her soft skin. He held her to him tightly, protecting her nakedness and shattered emotions. She sobbed into his rich blond hair and gripped the lapels of his coat.

"Don't...go," she begged, all her noble intentions destroyed by grief. "Whatever's wrong...I love you."

He buried his face in her dark hair. "I love you, too." His hands shaking, Ethan gently pulled her slip and bra back into place, then wound his arms around her and wrapped her even closer to his chest. "Shhh. We'll be all right," he crooned with all the confidence he could manage.

Slowly she got herself under control. Tara drew back a little and nuzzled her face against his. He kissed the wet streaks on her cheeks, then reached into his coat pocket and retrieved a linen handkerchief. "Remember when we met that day in Washington?" he teased her gruffly. "You were crying, and I gave you my handkerchief. You were very proper and insisted on returning it."

She nodded and gave him a tiny, sad smile. "And you said, "'Well, I can't take it back, because it has makeup on it. What would my mother think?'"

"But you returned it anyway. Keep this one," Ethan whispered.

She nodded again, her eyes full of sadness. He helped her slip into her blouse, then fumbled with the tiny buttons, his big fingers having trouble with the delicate task. She started to help him, but he shook his head. "Let me," he said hoarsely. "I want to remember how everything about you feels."

That heartfelt remark made her cover her face with her hands. Ethan murmured husky, nearly incoherent words of reassurance as he finished with her blouse and carefully tucked it back into the pleated gray skirt she wore. He raised her chin with his forefinger and gently pressed the handkerchief to her eyes.

"You're going to remember me as looking awful," she noted matter-of-factly. "The curse of water-soluble make-up."

He shook his head, his expression tender. "No, Cinderella. You'll always be the most beautiful woman at the ball."

With a sound of sorrow, she rested her cheek against his shoulder and stroked trembling fingertips over his face, memorizing every feature. Ethan was deserting her out of loyalty to Logan, but she forced herself not to reveal her puzzlement and pain. The limousine's intercom buzzed. Ethan reached up and tapped the button. "Yes, Sam?" he asked wearily.

"I hate to interrupt, sir, but we're running short on time."

"Thanks. We'll go in a moment."

The intercom clicked off. Tara grasped Ethan's broad shoulders convulsively and steeled herself not to cry anymore. She understood why Logan was important to him, she kept telling herself. She knew all the idealistic plans he had to honor. Her face still pressed against his coat, she spoke in a muffled, choked voice. "I'm not going to look at you or kiss you goodbye. That's the only way I can leave without making us both feel worse."

His arms tightened around her harshly. "Love you," he whispered. "Four weeks isn't a very long time."

"We've never been apart more than a few days. And *those* were long times."

Gulping for breath, Tara slid out of his lap, grabbed her purse from where it rested on the floorboard and twisted quickly toward the door. She shoved it open and started out, her head bent with control. She put one hand back, intending to push herself up. Ethan clasped the hand in a hard grip.

For a heartbreaking moment Tara sat still, her back to him, her head still down, her hand squeezing his in one last, tormented goodbye. Then she pulled away and vaulted out of the limousine. A startled Sam arrived to take her arm. He shut the limo's door and held her elbow as she stepped up on the curb.

Tara turned toward him and grasped his shoulder. She knew that Sam had been Ethan's personal driver for a long time. He'd started back in Kentucky, when Ethan was CEO at Allied Foods. "He's upset, Sam," she said in a voice that broke. "Stay with him until he gets on the plane, if you can."

"I will, Ms. Ross. God bless you for caring so much about him."

She nodded, unable to say more. Tara hurried through the stream of impersonal humanity on the sidewalk and back into her office building. The cool silence of the lobby draped over her as she stood, staring down at her hands. She'd lost Ethan's handkerchief.

Her eyes full of new tears, she ran back outside. The limousine had disappeared in traffic. She stumbled among people, searching the sidewalk for the beautiful linen square bearing Ethan's monogram. Finally, her shoulders slumped, Tara slowly walked inside again. She felt as if Ethan were never coming back.

Tara knew that the apartment Maggie kept in the elegant old building was only one of the homes she maintained both in the States and abroad, but she also knew that Maggie was still in New York. So Tara sat down on a bench near the

doorman's post and waited. She had the freedom to be per
sistent, since McGee was having dinner tonight with a group
of his former co-workers at the network.

Midnight came and went. The doorman chatted with her,
brought her a soft drink, showed her photographs of hi
grandchildren. At 1:00 a.m. a beetle-shaped yellow ca
stopped at the curb, and Maggie, dressed in a fortune'
worth of rubies and a taffeta gown that matched her re
hair, made an impressive exit. When she saw Tara, she gri
maced and looked guilty.

Tara stood and walked toward her, arching one brow i
rebuke. "You've been avoiding me," she said flatly. "I'v
called you five times."

"Hmm. Would you believe that I've been embroiled in
hot affair with an Arab sheikh?"

"No. I *would* believe, however, that there are things abou
Logan Tobacco and Ethan that you don't want to tell me
Things that happened since last week at the restaurant."

Maggie sighed in defeat and, looking grim, gestured to
ward her building. "Let's go have a stiff drink."

Seated in Maggie's plush art nouveau living room, Tar
forced down a swallow of brandy and riveted her gaze o
Maggie's back. Maggie stood at a window, looking down o
the traffic far below them.

"Talk," Tara ordered her. She had to understand wh
Ethan had left her. "Dammit, you've always been straigh
with me. Don't stop now. What's been happening wit
Ethan and the Logan board?"

Maggie pressed the cool lip of her brandy snifter to he
forehead. "I find men to be some of the most distastefu
creatures in the evolutionary order, you know," she mut
tered. "Oh, there are a few noble ones, I suppose. I was i
love with one once. I'm twenty-nine years old. Do you thin
I'll ever find one worth having?"

"I think," Tara said between clenched teeth, "that you're evading the issue."

"No, Tara, the lack of noble males in the world is *precisely* the issue." She paused. "When Ethan came to your aid in front of the board members, he erased any doubt they had about the nature of his relationship with you. It was obvious to anyone with two eyes that you love each other."

Tara set her brandy glass on a table and clasped her hands together. Her fingers were icy cold. "And?"

"And they grilled Ethan about it. We had a special executive meeting. It was hell for him."

Tara's hands rose to her throat in fear. "How did he handle it?"

Maggie's voice lashed out, full of sarcasm. "*Beautifully.* Isn't that what you'd expect from Ethan?"

Tara stood, dread curdling the blood in her veins. She walked over to Maggie and grasped her arm roughly. "What do you mean?"

When Maggie turned to face her, Tara saw that she had tears on her cheeks. Maggie clasped her shoulders and looked at her sympathetically. "I mean that the only way he could save himself was to tell them that he's no longer seeing you."

Tara stepped back, shaking her head. Disbelief and horror made her feel dizzy. "It was just a bluff."

"I hope so, sweetie, I really do." Maggie put an arm around her as she swayed. "Sit down."

Tara stared at her shrewdly. "Is that why you weren't going to tell me about it?"

"Yes...and...I thought that if he *wasn't* bluffing the board, he'd have the good sense to change his mind while you two were apart."

"You *know* Ethan. You know he—"

"Nobody really knows Ethan," Maggie said in a sorrowful voice. "He can put an impenetrable shield around his privacy. I suppose he learned to do that because of the ugly way he grew up.''

"*I* know him," Tara protested desperately. "He wouldn't stop seeing me because the board—''

"I cornered him in his office after the meeting to ask him if he really meant it. He wouldn't talk to me, Tara. I yelled and carried on in my best style while he just stood there, staring out the window. Finally, he called that Dora person, his little protector, into the office and had her stand there until I marched out.''

Tara hugged her stomach and ducked her head, fighting the nausea that overwhelmed her. Ethan, no! she thought raggedly. "Did he really have to go abroad?" she gasped.

"Oh, Logan *does* have legitimate business to conduct outside the country.''

Tara gritted her teeth. "Dammit, Maggie, did he—''

"No, sweetie," Maggie answered in a gentle, resigned voice. "The president, Barkley Stewart, could have gone. Any number of vice presidents could have gone.''

"Oh, God, Maggie, then he just did it to put some distance between us." She felt as if she were strangling. She spoke the next words simply to give form to her worst fear. It would take a long time for her to believe them. "Ethan had to choose between Logan and me. And I lost.''

Maggie led her to a couch and they sat down together, Maggie's arm still around her shoulders. "You're going to stay in one of my guest rooms tonight.''

"No...no." Tara shut her eyes. "I have to go home." In a haze of shock, she struggled for a moment to remember why going home was so important. "McGee needs me.''

"Ethan needs you, too," Maggie replied in a thoughtful tone. "Don't ever stop believing that.''

Tara shook her head. "But there's no way we can be together as long as he's at Logan." Shivering, she looked at Maggie despondently. "Getting the company out of the tobacco business has become his Holy Grail, and—'' her voice was a tortured rasp "—anyone who gets in the way... has to... go." She stopped, fighting for control. "Even me."

McGee's weakened condition kept him from being a graceful drunk. From her bed, Tara listened to him bumble through the living room, ouching when he ran into a piece of furniture, chuckling when he thumped the wall. He was happy, she noted with vague approval. For the first time since he'd gotten back he seemed to feel good. Tara waited, listening distractedly, hoping that she wouldn't have to get up and help him to the master bedroom.

Silence descended, and she knew that he was trying to tiptoe. Abruptly the half-open door to the guest room swung back. His tall body banged the door frame, then lounged against it loosely, outlined by the glow from the lamp she'd left on in the living room.

"Hey, Rossy!" he whispered loudly. "You awake, kid?"

The way she felt at this moment, Tara didn't expect to sleep anytime soon, perhaps not for years. Still dressed in the slacks and white top she'd worn to meet Maggie, she lay on the narrow guest bed, her back propped against the headboard. "Yes, McGee, I'm awake."

"Good." He shuffled in and plopped down cross-legged on the floor beside her bed. He reached up and patted her knee companionably. "Hey, what kinda nightie is this?"

"I'm still dressed, McGee. You're mauling my slacks."

He chortled, rested both forearms on the side of the bed and propped his chin on them. "I had a great time tonight, Rossy."

"The guys will be glad to have you back on the job."

"Don't know if I'm going back to work for the network. Might do something else. Life's too short, you know."

"I know," she whispered in a tired, small voice.

"Hey, kid, I wish we could have made it work. You and me."

Tara reached out and patted his head affectionately. "We couldn't."

"I know that now. But we had a helluva good time trying."

"You were always a...a comet, McGee. All fire and lovely dazzle. I'm a...mm...a quiet, stable planet."

He laughed. "Boy, where'd you pick up a weird astronomy analogy like that?"

From Ethan, she realized abruptly. Tara pressed her fingertips to her mouth and squinted her eyes shut as a wave of new pain washed over her. She'd thought that she'd hurt all that she could hurt, for tonight.

"Kid?" McGee said anxiously. "Rossy?" Now that he'd settled beside her bed, he seemed to be getting sober. "What are you doing here in the dark in all your clothes? Hell, the bed's still made up."

She shook her head fiercely, rebuking herself for the shudders that racked her body, regardless. Tara slid down on the bedspread and turned on her side, facing away from him with her hands still against her mouth. He wobbled to his feet and sat down beside her, then put a comforting hand on her shoulder.

"Spill your guts, kid. I'm no mind reader, but I'm not so dense that I haven't figured out that something's been eating at you for days."

Tara fought the need to tell him about Ethan, afraid she'd hurt him despite his nonchalant words about their past relationship. "It's nothing," she whispered.

"Come on, Rossy," he growled in a teasing but reproachful voice. "I'm still your buddy, okay? Want me to guess? Uhh... You've been watching too many bleach commercials on TV and you're upset because *you'll* never get your socks whiter than white. Or—let's see.... You're depressed because the pro football season is still a couple weeks away. Me, too." He paused, and his voice became serious. "Or... you've got man trouble, and the man ain't me."

"Oh, McGee."

"Aha. Bingo."

"I tried not to... get involved...."

"I know that, Rossy. I worried about you the whole time I was away, because I figured you'd set up some sort of shrine to me and ignore the rest of the world. In a selfish way, I wanted you to."

Tara sighed deeply and turned to lie on her back. He kept his hand on her shoulder. "It was the least I could do."

"And I appreciate it. Now... quit stalling and tell me about this guy."

Tara reached up and grasped his hand. "All right," she murmured, feeling almost relieved. At least she could stop pretending around McGee now. Now that she and Ethan no longer had anything to pretend about. Her voice low and hoarse, she began to talk.

What was the name of that sentimental old song? "Autumn in New York"? Yes, that was it. Tara stood outside the posh Manhattan hotel, frowning at the line of oak saplings set in large ornamental containers along the sidewalk. Their golden leaves rustled in the cool, evening breeze. The song, she thought doggedly. How did the lyrics go? Oh, yes, it was something about how romantic New York was in autumn. She chuckled bitterly. According to Maggie, Ethan had returned today. There was *nothing* romantic about autumn in New York.

"Hypnotizing trees again, are you?" McGee said drolly. He had just finished paying their cabdriver. "Get a move on, Rossy. Never be late for an awards dinner where you're getting dinner *and* an award."

"The irony of this event overwhelms me," she told McGee in a sardonic voice as they made their way through the hotel lobby. The annual banquet held by the National Medical Writers' Association celebrated its members' achievements during the past year. And her achievement was Best Investigative Series, for her stories about Logan Tobacco's medical experts.

She sat dutifully through the dinner, making all the right small talk, doing all the polite things without paying much attention, which had become her general approach to life during the past four weeks. The knowledge that Ethan had probably deserted her was now a cold wall around her feelings for him. Putting up walls was the only way she could survive.

She collected her award, went back to her seat and sat down beside McGee. A svelte blond woman had been winking at him across the table all evening, and Tara suspected that he'd been winking back. Ah, yes, McGee was ready to leave the nest, Tara thought with tender amusement.

He put one arm around her. "I'm proud of you, kid. But that award looks like a fat angel perched on a hamburger bun."

"It's a sort of *Winged Victory*, you oaf," she grumbled. Tara handed it to him. "Now I can escape to the ladies' rest room for a while."

"You okay, kid?"

She looked at him without even attempting to hide her misery. "No. But I'll live."

Tara left the banquet room and crossed the hotel's mezzanine. She started down a long, empty hallway, peering at door after door without success. The hotel's architects had been paid a great deal of money to hide the women's lounge so well, she thought ruefully. The soft sound of footsteps behind her made the hair rise on the back of her neck. Deserted hall, she noted nervously. And here she was, alone.

She kept her stride casual but walked a little faster. The rhythm of the stranger's footsteps picked up immediately.

Tara rounded a corner and stopped, dismayed when she saw that she had blundered into a dead end bordered on three sides by the closed doors of unused banquet rooms. She whipped around, her senses straining. The stranger was still coming her way, and she was trapped.

Tara glanced down at the tiny silver purse that matched her shimmering cocktail dress. Ordinarily, she'd have a lethal nail file and her security whistle, but not tonight. But she didn't need a weapon, not for physical defense, at any rate. Because the tuxedoed stranger who stepped around the corner was Ethan.

Twelve

He continued to come toward her. Stunned, she stepped back. He stopped, frowning in concern over her evasive movement. Tara noted swiftly that he looked older, thinner, more tired than she'd ever seen him before. But in his black tuxedo he was still the most devastating picture of masculine appeal in the world, and she knew that no other man would ever hold her attention the way he could. All the weeks of missing him, of worrying about him, pooled inside her as a painful ache.

"What are you doing here?" she asked gruffly.

"I just got back today. I heard about the awards banquet, and I made arrangements to attend. I knew it was the only way I could see you."

"Safely," she amended. "The only way you could see me safely, in public."

"What the hell?" he said in a hoarse, disbelieving tone. He put his hands out, urging her to come to him. What was wrong with her? he thought numbly. Why was she looking at him as if she didn't want to be there? All the loneliness, all the planning he had gone through over the past four weeks had focused on the moment when he could come back to her. And now something was horribly wrong.

She shook her head with a weak, vague motion. "I'm just as tired as you are of hiding from the world. I wish you hadn't come here."

Frowning harder, Ethan started to tell her that they didn't need to hide anymore. But a sudden thought killed his announcement before it could form in his throat. "How's McGee?" he asked slowly.

"Still living at my place."

Ethan fought to keep from wincing openly. "I saw him at the table with you tonight. He's looking better."

"He used to be a handsome man. When he gains a little more weight, he will be, again."

"And?" Ethan let the word hang.

She'd make it easy for him to keep his distance, Tara thought sadly. "And . . . we'll see."

"Do you love him?" he asked bluntly.

After all the reassurances she'd given Ethan about *not* loving McGee, Tara was astonished that he thought that. Or else . . . Ethan was looking for an easy, guilt-free exit, and knowing that she was back in McGee's arms would provide one.

"I don't know yet. Anything's possible."

He felt as if she'd slapped him. This couldn't be happening, Ethan told himself. He had left town to give her time to take care of McGee, not time to fall back in love with him. "Do you love him?" Ethan repeated fiercely.

Tara wavered, trembling all over. "Four weeks, Ethan," she said in a low, strained voice. "You left me for four weeks. You didn't even want to *talk* to me. I tried to understand . . . that you needed to protect yourself at Logan. But it hurt."

He advanced on her, his eyes glittering coldly and his hands clenched. She didn't retreat this time, and he stopped only inches from her. "Damn...it," he said between clenched teeth. "Answer me. Do...you...love...McGee?"

He hadn't denied anything about his reason for leaving her. Logan Tobacco would always be between them, and she couldn't bear the thought, selfish as it was, that he would never choose her over the company. "Perhaps I do," she answered in a husky, tired tone.

All the anger seemed to drain out of him. "Oh, my God," he said softly. "I thought nothing could change the way you felt about me."

Tara didn't try to hold back tears any longer. She made no sound, but they slid down her cheeks. "I thought nothing could either." She paused, swallowing hard. "But it has." Logan, she added silently.

They stood, sharing their sorrow without words, two people who had found something unique, something blessed, and then lost it. "I trusted you," he managed finally.

Tara laughed with a soft, bitter tone. "And I trusted you. I trusted you to love me more than anything in the world."

And I do, Ethan thought. You'll never know how much. "I suppose," he said in a cool voice, "that the only important point is that you've decided to stay with McGee."

She couldn't answer him, couldn't even nod. All the emotion drained out of her, and she gazed up at Ethan with silent acceptance. She had lost him, and her life would never be the same.

"All right, then," he whispered, his eyes hooded with control. "But never forget that I'm a thief at heart. I can't promise that I won't try to steal you back from McGee."

A gallant lie, she thought. "Good luck...with...Logan," Tara murmured brokenly.

Ethan couldn't bring himself to tell her the news he'd been saving since before he'd left for China. It didn't matter anymore, because she wanted to stay with McGee. Ethan turned and walked away, his stride unhurried. After all, he had nowhere important to go, and no one worth going to.

* * *

"And so... it's time that I left, Rossy."

McGee's announcement came at the end of a long, thoughtful discussion over dinner in her dining room. Tara leaned back in her chair, took a long swallow of the champagne he'd bought and squinted. She was just past tipsy.

"You know, McGee, the last time I got drunk, I was eighteen years old." She raised her fluted glass in a toast. "Once a decade is my limit. I believe tonight's the night, for this decade."

He reached over and patiently took the glass away from her. "Kid, the sight of you soused would be either hilarious or tragic. I suspect that in your current state of mind it would be the latter case. Cool it."

She looked at him apologetically. "I'm not trying to make you feel bad for deciding to move out. I'm happy for you."

"Ssssh. I know what—or, rather, *who*—your problem is. I won't pack up until you've gotten yourself on even ground again."

"That could take years," she quipped dryly. It was no joke, but she didn't tell McGee that. "So don't wait."

The buzz of the intercom startled them both. McGee went to the speaker unit in the kitchen. "Hi ya, Bill," Tara heard him greet the lobby guard in a boisterous tone. "I *told* you, no more visits from Raquel Welch! She's getting on my nerves!"

Smiling wearily, Tara propped her chin on her hands and listened to Bill's sputtering laugh. "I've got a beautiful lady down here, but it's not Raquel. It's someone named Maggie Logan, asking to see Ms. Ross."

Tara groaned. No more! she protested grimly. No more to do with Logan Tobacco or anyone connected to it. Not right now.

"Tell her I'll call her later," she instructed McGee.

"Tell her Ms. Ross will call her later," he relayed to Bill. "But if she's got good legs, *I'll* be right down."

"But the lady insists—" Bill began.

"Ms. Ross is getting drunk," McGee said politely. "And she prefers to throw up alone."

There was a commotion over the intercom. Maggie's sultry, annoyed voice burst over it. "Tara! You let me come up or I'll skin your head!"

Tara thumped the table with the flat of her hand. "Tell Maggie she's got five minutes."

"You can have five minutes with Tara, and two hours with me," McGee said wickedly. "Come on up, if you dare."

"Is this McGee Webster? Dammit, Webster—"

Tara heard McGee jauntily cut Maggie's voice off. He walked back into the dining room and stopped beside her, then squeezed her shoulder. Tara looked up at him ruefully to say, "You'd better retire to the safety of your bedroom until after Maggie leaves. She's violent when provoked."

Laughing, he nodded and left the room. They both knew that she wanted to talk with Maggie in private. A minute later she heard the door to the master bedroom shut. Chimes sounded, and Tara went to the door. She opened it and gave Maggie a patient look.

"Come in."

Maggie, wearing black leather boots with a matching miniskirt and jacket, breezed through the door and glared around, searching for McGee. "Where is he? I felt sorry for him that night he fainted at the restaurant, but he's obviously in fine form now. You didn't tell me he's a wisecracking flirt."

Tara shut the door. "Calm down. He just teased you the way he teases everyone else."

"I don't have time for that tonight!" Her mouth compressed in a grim line, Maggie turned swiftly to face Tara. "I have to talk to you about Ethan."

"I don't want to talk about Ethan—"

"Ethan resigned!"

Tara stared at her in open-mouthed shock. "W-when?"

"Weeks ago! He gave his resignation to Barkley Stewart before he left for China!"

Tara grabbed Maggie's shoulders. *"What?"*

Maggie grabbed her shoulders, too, and shook her lightly. "Stewart agreed not to announce it until Ethan came back home!" She shook her head. "You've got the *when* and the *what*, but don't ask me *why*. All I know is that Ethan resigned over a month ago!" She paused, grimacing with distress. "And he's gone."

"Where?" Tara said in a desperate voice.

"Reporters! Now you've added *where*! I don't know that either! No one knows. He's not at his house, and his personal Attila the Hun, Dora Brown, says he gave her an inscribed diamond bracelet as a parting gift but wouldn't even tell *her* where he was going."

Tara went over to the couch and sat down limply. Why hadn't Ethan told her he'd resigned? Why had he suffered through the past few weeks alone? And continued to suffer now, alone? Tara rubbed her temples, trying to think. "Where would he go? Where..." Kentucky. The cabin.

There was no way to call, because the cabin didn't have a phone. If he was at the cabin, maybe he didn't want to see her. Not after the things they'd said to each other. But she had to take that chance. She had to make sure that he was all right.

"Call the airport," she told Maggie. "Get me the next flight to Lexington, Kentucky." She ran to the door of the master bedroom and pounded it hurriedly. "McGee! I have to get my suitcase out of the closet!"

He opened the door tentatively and peered out at Maggie with coy expectation. "Is it safe?"

Maggie shook her fist at him. "Come out, you heathen."

Tara pushed past McGee into the room, leaving him to joust verbally with Maggie. All she cared about was finding Ethan, and answers, as soon as she could.

* * *

The cicadas sang a whirring chorus that rose and fell in the cool September morning. The sun had only recently burned a chilly dew off the mountains, but now its heat offered a last hint of summer. Cutting firewood was warm work, and Ethan removed his flannel shirt. He kept his red cloth suspenders on, because his scarred jeans were a little loose around the waist these days. The suspenders clung to the sweating, straining muscles of his chest and back as he rhythmically swung his ax.

Cutting firewood. That seemed to be his only goal, the only chore mindless enough to let him grieve while he worked. He had given up Logan and lost Tara. Without Logan he had dignity. Without Tara he had no dignity at all. He was going to win her back, somehow. He didn't yet have a plan, but he knew that he'd try. He could live with the fact that she didn't love him as much as he loved her, he told himself grimly as he worked. There would never be another woman who was so special, who could make him feel so complete.

The thick log cracked in two, and Ethan wearily propped the ax against one of the halves. Wiping his face with the back of his hand, he left the growing woodpile behind the cabin and walked around front, his thick brogans sinking into loamy soil made wet by autumn rains.

His eyes flickered over the panorama of Kentucky mountains, and he tried to conjure the sweet sense of home that usually came to him in this place. When his gaze reached the curving, rutted road in the valley below, he froze. A quarter-mile away, an unmistakable figure in jeans and a white windbreaker slipped on the muddy road, fell to one knee, then stood up again. Tara.

Shocked, bewildered, desperately glad to see her for whatever reason, Ethan left the cabin's yard at a fast, swinging walk. She had her head down so she could watch the muddy ground cautiously, but when she heard his footsteps, she glanced up. Ethan slowed his walk as he approached her, searching her expression for clues to her emotions. He saw relief in her eyes. And when he stopped, facing her from only a foot away, he saw the shimmer of tears.

"I thought you'd be here. I had to make sure you were all right," she murmured.

Disappointment made his voice a little sharp. "Your sense of duty is noted." Ethan sighed. "Why are you on foot?"

"I couldn't find anything with four-wheel drive to rent, and the car I rented instead would never survive this road. So I left it at the main road and walked."

He glanced at her sweaty, tired face, then down at her mud-covered jogging shoes. She'd struggled to get here, and he wished he could tell her how much that meant to him. She carried no purse or luggage. "I'll give you a ride back in the Jeep," he ventured. "I assume you can't stay long. Taking a Friday off on my account? I appreciate it."

She didn't answer but looked up at him shrewdly, frowning. "Can I have a drink of water?"

"Certainly." He gestured toward the cabin and took her elbow in a helpful grip. They walked back to the cabin's yard, side by side, a gossamer silence trapping too many questions between them. She sat down on a broad, smooth stump near the front door and waited while he went inside. He came back and handed her a plastic cup filled with cold water from the well behind the cabin.

"Thanks." She drank deeply, glad for anything that distracted her from the intensity of his watchful blue eyes.

"So you heard about my resignation," he said bluntly. "Maggie must have told you."

Tara nodded and set the cup down. The soft tone of her voice belied the turmoil inside her. "I don't understand it. I don't understand *anything*, Ethan."

He stood over her, his hands on his hips, looking down at her with a matter-of-fact expression. "Logan is expanding its foreign markets, and there's nothing I can do about it. I did what the board wanted me to do, which was to settle the negotiations. But I turned in my resignation first."

Tara's hands clenched in her lap. "Why didn't you tell me that before you left for China?"

"And complicate your life with McGee? Make you feel that you *had* to tell him about us? Make you feel sorry for me? I didn't want to do that to you." He paused, and his voice became cold. "I don't want you to feel sorry for me now."

"You let me think that you were simply trying to break off our relationship." Tara noted that his eyes filled with surprise. She nodded in order to emphasize her words. "That's what I thought. That you had chosen Logan over me. I learned that you told the board you were no longer seeing me...and I...decided that you weren't bluffing. That Logan would always take precedence over our relationship."

"Oh, God," he said wearily. "None of that was true." Ethan ran a hand through his hair and exhaled. "All I wanted was to get out of the way so that you could take care of McGee without worrying about me."

She chuckled hoarsely. "You didn't think I'd worry when you left the country for a month? When you didn't even want to talk to me on the phone while you were away?"

He shook his head almost imperceptibly, his eyes full of pain. "I thought you were all wrapped up in McGee's problems."

"I was." Tara bent forward and steepled her hands around her face. Staring at the ground, she quivered with sorrow. "But that didn't mean I wanted to fall in love with him again."

Ethan gestured vaguely, summing up all their regrets, and stared at the serene mountains beyond them, trying to clear the blur from his eyes. "Well," he managed in a hoarse voice, "I suppose I can understand how easy it was for sympathy to become romance."

Tara tilted her head back and gazed at him angrily. Her hands fell in her lap. "You don't understand *anything*."

Ethan cleared his throat. "Hate me for asking this, but are you and McGee—"

"No."

His lips parted in surprise. "Why not?"

She shook both fists at him. "Do you think I could ever stop loving you? Do you honestly believe that in a month's time I could forget everything you mean to me and go to bed with McGee? Oh, Ethan!"

"You told me that you love McGee!"

"I said *perhaps* I love McGee. I wanted to give you an easy out! I thought that's what you wanted to hear!"

"*Do* you love him?"

She vaulted to her feet, shaking, her voice fierce. "Of course not! McGee is getting ready to move out! He's flirting with other women! He's a terrific man and I'll always care about him, but I'll always *love* you!"

Tara froze, knowing that her confession had just made her more vulnerable than she'd ever been before. She waited desperately, gazing at Ethan. He studied her with an incredulous look in his eyes. Then, slowly, his rugged face softened into the most heart-stopping expression of relief and devotion.

"You just made my life perfect," he whispered.

Tara cried out in bittersweet happiness as his arms went around her in a fierce, possessive embrace. He pulled her tightly to his chest, her hands crushed against hard muscle and downy, damp hair. "What am I going to do about you?" she asked with gentle rebuke. "You gave up one of the most powerful corporate positions in the world, and you couldn't care less." She shook her head in mock dismay.

He smiled crookedly. "I have a clean conscience, and I have you."

"You have me," she repeated, nodding. "You can count on that."

They barely got inside the cabin doorway before all the weeks of loneliness and desire took reason away. Somewhere in the midst of kissing each other fervently, they settled on the rough, plank floor just beyond the doorstep. The world was a haven of caresses and sweet tears. Neither of them minded the coarse surface under their bodies; neither even noticed it.

They loved each other with a gentle wildness that ended quickly in soft moans. They were naked, sweaty, grimy, and thoroughly ecstatic as he carried her through the cabin and out the back door. By the well, they washed each other with cold water, shivering and laughing with giddy delight. Then they curled up together on the bed, talking between kisses, exploring each other's bodies with uninhibited intimacy. They made love again, this time so slowly that the pleasure crested, plateaued, then spiraled into a realm that left them holding each other in silent, trembling amazement.

Facing each other, they lay on their sides. Ethan brushed his fingertips across her flushed complexion and never looked away from her glowing eyes. He told her about his weeks abroad, everything he'd said and done and thought as he'd prepared to leave Logan. He told her about beautiful sights he'd seen in China, places that the two of them would visit, together, someday.

Her fingers gently caressing his mouth, Tara related McGee's progress through the weeks and his intention not to return to his career as a network cameraman. Then, her voice throaty, she told him how McGee had reacted to the knowledge that she'd fallen in love with someone else while he was in Lebanon.

"I was wrong to feel guilty," she told Ethan. "I realize that now."

"We've both learned a lot about ourselves," he murmured gently. "Think what would have happened if you and I had never met. We'd both still be driven, uptight bachelors."

"We're both still bachelors," she reminded him coyly.

"Not for long."

She kissed him tenderly. "Is that a proposal?"

His eyes shut, Ethan nuzzled his mouth against hers as he spoke. "Still want those kids, that house with the big yard, that membership in the PTA?"

She laughed softly. "Oh, yes."

"How would you like a college student for a husband?"

"Only if he's one of those sexy, scientific types. Perhaps...hmm...an astronomy major."

"That can be arranged."

He pulled the covers over them and they fell into an exhausted, happy sleep, snuggled together spoon-style. As the ethereal magenta shadows of dusk crept over them, she woke him up with wanton caresses. Chuckling, Tara settled on top of his body and took him while he was smiling sleepily. He never opened his eyes, but his smile grew broader and a light sweat broke on his forehead. Afterward they propped themselves on pillows and watched the last moments of a glorious sunset beyond the cabin window.

He kept her close by his side, his arm around her shoulders. Tara curled one leg over him and burrowed her face into the crook of his neck. "Ethan," she murmured languidly. "I forgot to tell you. I've beaten my cigarette demon for good. It's gone."

"I've beaten mine, too." They shared a pensive laugh. She tilted her head back and smiled at him. He smiled back but arched one brow at her. "I'm proud of you, but if you have a relapse, I'll understand. I hate to use the cliché...but old habits die hard."

"You and I know that only too well, don't we?"

Ethan nodded, understanding. They'd had to overcome so many stubborn problems before they could cherish this peace. He touched her face gently, his eyes gleaming, and whispered, "Think of all the wonderful *new* habits we're going to form."

Her kiss promised a lifetime of them.

* * * * *

ATTRACTIVE, SPACE SAVING BOOK RACK

Display your most prized novels on this handsome and sturdy book rack. The hand-rubbed walnut finish will blend into your library decor with quiet elegance, providing a practical organizer for your favorite hard-or soft-covered books.

Only $9.95

Approximately 16" x 8" when assembled

Assembles in seconds!

To order, rush your name, address and zip code, along with a check or money order for $10.70* ($9.95 plus 75¢ postage and handling) payable to *Silhouette Books.*

Silhouette Desire

COMING NEXT MONTH

#433 WITH ALL MY HEART—Annette Broadrick
As soon as he saw beautiful, reserved Emily Hartman, charismatic Jeremy
Jones knew they were from two different worlds. Could he find a way to
join their disparate lives?

#434 HUSBAND FOR HIRE—Raye Morgan
Workaholic Charity Ames needed a temporary husband—fast! After
taking the job, Ross Carpenter's ulterior motives were soon forgotten.
This husband-for-hire wanted to be permanent!

#435 CROSSFIRE—Naomi Horton
Eleven years ago Kailin Yarbro had told Brett Douglass she was pregnant.
He'd known she was lying—but now she was back, and there was a
child....

#436 SAVANNAH LEE—Noreen Brownlie
Savannah Lee had promised to tame Blake Elliot's cats to prove that her
cat obedience school was legitimate. Blake hadn't counted on her feline
expertise taming *his* tomcat tendencies.

#437 GOLDILOCKS AND THE BEHR—Lass Small
When Angus Behr discovered "Goldilocks" sleeping in his bed, he knew
he wasn't going to be able to let Hillary Lambert go—this she-Behr was
just right.

#438 USED-TO-BE LOVERS—Linda Lael Miller
The powerful chemistry that had united Tony Morelli and Sharon
Harrison with heart-stopping passion had turned into an explosive
situation. Could they find a loving solution?

AVAILABLE NOW:

TALES OF THE RISING MOON
A Desire trilogy by Joyce Thies

MOON OF THE RAVEN—June

Conlan Fox was part American Indian and as tough
as the Montana land he rode, but it took fragile yet
strong-willed Kerry Armstrong to make his dreams
come true.

REACH FOR THE MOON—August

It would take a heart of stone for Steven Armstrong
to evict the woman and children living on his land.
But when Steven met Samantha, eviction was the
last thing on his mind!

GYPSY MOON—October

Robert Armstrong met Serena when he returned to
his ancestral estate in Connecticut. Their fiery
temperaments clashed from the start, but despite
himself, Rob was falling under the Gypsy's spell.

Don't miss any of Joyce Thies's enchanting
TALES OF THE RISING MOON,
coming to you from Silhouette Desire.

SD 432